PULP Literature

PULP *Literature*

PULP LITERATURE PRESS

Issue No. 20, Autumn 2018

Pulp Literature Press, Publisher; Jennifer Landels, Managing Editor; Melanie Anastasiou, Acquisitions Editor; Susan Pieters, Story Editor; Jessica Fabrizius, Assistant Editor; Daniel Cowper, Poetry Editor; Emily Osborne, Poetry Editor; Amanda Bidnall, Copy Editor & Graphic Designer; Mary Rykov, Proofreader; Kris Sayer, Graphic Designer. For advertising rates, direct inquiries to info@ pulpliterature.com.

Cover painting, Jinn, by Ben Baldwin. Illustration for 'Away Game' by John Henry Friesen. All other illustrations by Mel Anastasiou.

Pulp Literature: ISSN 2292-2164 (Print), ISSN 2292-2172 (Online), Issue No. 20, Autumn 2018.

Published quarterly by Pulp Literature Press, 21955 16 Ave, Langley BC, Canada V2Z 1K5, pulpliterature.com, at $15.00 per copy. Annual subscription $50.00 in Canada, $66.00 in continental USA, $82.00 elsewhere. Printed in Victoria, BC, Canada, by First Choice Books/Victoria Bindery. Copyright © 2018 Pulp Literature Press. All stories and works of art copyright © 2018 their authors as per bylines.

Pulp Literature Press gratefully acknowledges the support of the Canada Council for the Arts.

Pulp Literature is a proud member of the Magazine Association of BC and Magazines Canada.

TABLE OF CONTENTS

FROM THE PULP LIT PULPIT

A Score for Cross-Genre Fiction

Twenty issues in, the editors at *Pulp Literature* are feeling victorious. Launched five years ago on Kickstarter, we have proven to be the little magazine that could. When people told us that we had to limit ourselves to a single genre category, we disagreed. We three editors love to read the best works in every genre and find a variety of fiction on our nightstands, from mystery to fantasy to literary to romance. So we trusted in intelligent readers who feel the same way and love to read widely across the spectrum of fiction flavours. And here we are! Bravo!

Enjoy these fabulous stories, an array of fiction unlike any other magazine we've seen out there. And if you approve of us, don't let your applause be silent. Recommend us to friends, subscribe or gift subscribe through our website, and become our friends on Patreon. Join us on our journey through the next twenty issues … and beyond.

Jen, Mel, Sue & Jess
Pulp Literature Press

Issue 20's featured author, **Kristene Perron**, asks us to savour the simple things in life and question the validity of tradition in 'Flavour of the Forsaken'.

Those of you who admire magpies for their intelligence and unique beauty will find these qualities in this year's winners of the Magpie Award for Poetry, **Kelli Allen**, **Christine Levickzy Riek**, and **Angela Caravan**.

Great-Great-Grandpa stops by for a visit 90 years after his death in 'Away Game' by **Mitchell Toews**, and for some reason, we're not at all surprised.

'Gross Motor' by **Sara Mang** takes us back to kindergarten, while the hardworking folks in Mitchell's Crossing contend with a nosy superhero and government officials in 'Small Town Superhero' by **Dave Beynon**.

Epiphany Ferrell exposes the dubious talents of a ne'er-do-well townsman in 'Every Town Has One', and **Susan Pieters** challenges us to walk in someone else's shoes with 'Waking Up Black'.

Love jewellery? We doubt you'll want one of the bracelets in **Summer Jewel Keown's** 'Indebted'.

Alex Reece Abbott lands quick punches you won't flinch from with 'Alphabet Soup', while coffee lovers and dreamers beware of 'The Hub', SiWC's Honourable Mention by **Erin Evans**.

Mel Anastasiou's graphic story 'Meat' involves a gargoyle who rises above his station, while **JM Landels**'s next instalment of *Allaigna's Song: Aria* takes us deeper into unknown territory.

GOOD BOOKS
for the price of a beer
Short stories, poetry, and comics you can't put down.

PULP Literature
pulpliterature.com

PULP Literature
Matthew Hughes
'The Devil You Don't'
Mel Anastasiou
Carolyn Oliver
Eric Del Carlo
FJ Bergmann
Anat Rabkin
Allaigna's Song: Aria

FLAVOUR OF THE FORSAKEN

Kristene Perron

Kristene Perron *has been shot, stabbed, drowned, run over and thrown from a building. During her ten years as a professional stunt woman, she learned all the interesting ways a person can get injured or die and then applied this unique education to her fiction. She is the co-author of the adventure science fiction series* Warpworld, *the 2010 winner of the Surrey International Writers' Conference Storyteller Award, and a 2015 Writers of the Future finalist. Her stories have appeared in* Escape Pod, Denizens of Darkness, Canadian Storyteller Magazine, The Barbaric Yawp, *and* Hemispheres Magazine. *Her friends wish she would stop talking about cats. You can find bits of Kristene on Twitter as @KristenePerron, on Facebook as @warpworld, or on Warpworld.ca.*

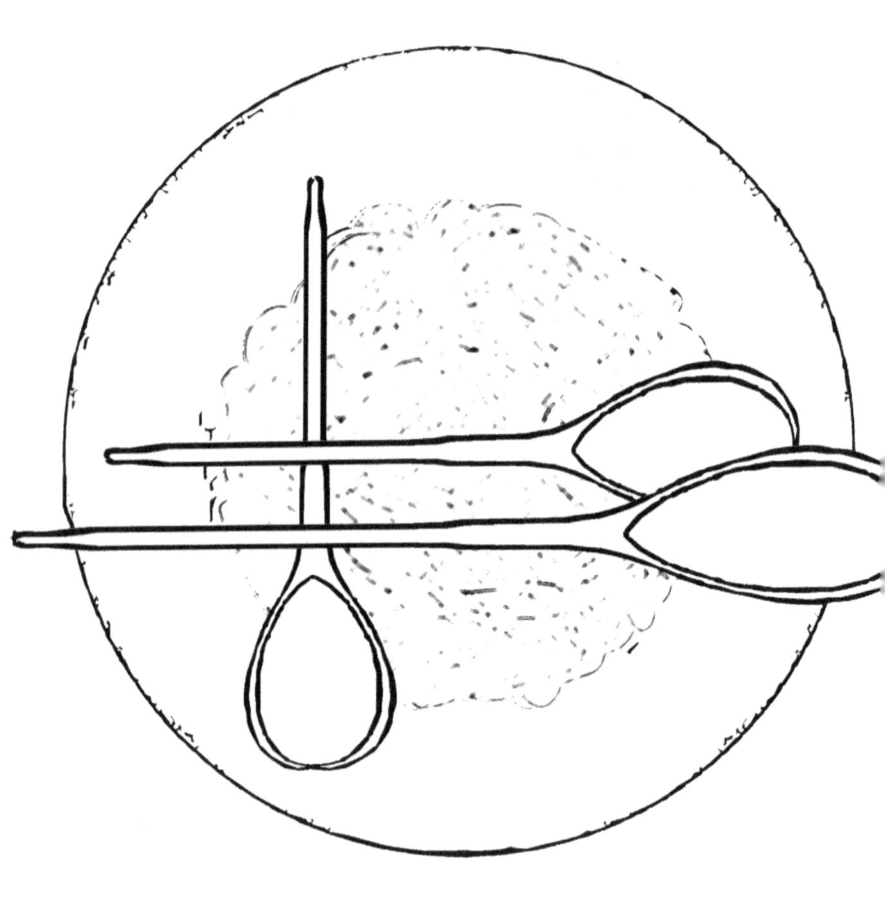

Flavour of the Forsaken

"You're going to end up bleeding in the gutter."

Pempasigle heard Makineng's words as he rolled to one side and wiped the blood from his face. Dribbles of morning light punctuated his shame. Right now, his friend was in a warm kitchen, exactly where he should have been.

No gutter. The bandits had taken him out to the alley to beat him senseless. Only crimson mud, urine, and old wash-water here.

"You were wrong," he wheezed, and then started to cry.

Empty pockets, he knew before he even found the strength to search. He searched anyway, his fingers digging down to the very corners, pulling out only wet lint and mushy crumbs. That would be enough; his hunger was not of the belly. After separating the crumbs from the lint, he forced them through swollen lips and onto his tongue.

Sweet haval sugar and the barest hint of sharpness. Fresh morning mint. The mint would have been picked before sunrise, before the sun licked the moisture from the leaves. His mother had taught him how to find the best morning mint in the market, to look for the leaves that had not curled at the edges. Home.

"They get everything?"

Pempasigle opened his eyes — he had not realized he had closed them — and saw a pair of heavy boots inches away. He followed the boots up to a leather longcoat, up to a head as big as a large pumpkin, up to a pair of yellow eyes, up to a shock of muddy green hair, up to a set of horns sweeping from back to front in an s-curve. Up to a Prang. The same Prang he had spotted shortly after his arrival. The same Prang the bandits who had befriended and tricked him had joked about.

Before he could answer, the Prang's mouth twisted. "Yeah, they got everything. Go home, City."

The boots departed in a slurp and suck of mud.

A Prang. Unthinkable. While not deemed unclean by the temple priests, no upright citizen would associate with such brutes. But what other options were left to him?

"Wait!" Pempasigle called. Pain of all varieties flared and throbbed and stabbed as he climbed out of the muck and onto hands and knees. The cursed ground did its best to hold him, but he yanked his hands free and stood, shaking his arms to rid himself of the crimson slop. "Wait!"

The boots did not pause. The woman wearing the boots did not look back.

Woman would not have been his guess if he had not heard the bandits' vulgar comments. Not exactly woman, either. Prangs could be male or female or both. Or neither? Pempasigle did not know. He had never seen a real Prang before yesterday.

"I need your help," he called.

The boots walked on, turned a corner, and disappeared.

"You're crazy," Makineng had said the day Pempasigle had told her of his plan to travel to the Margin.

The first rays of sun, skipping through the windows of the great house kitchen, caught the fine particles of flour in the air and illuminated multicoloured baskets of fresh fruit and vegetables. Heat from the bread ovens made this the best place to be on cold winter mornings. This was also the best time and place for a private conversation with Makineng, and so he had spent a week working up the courage to share his secret.

In those imagined conversations, Makineng had been concerned but supportive. This conversation had taken a different path. "If your head was a fruit and I cut it open, only fanciful dreams would spill out," Makineng said. She held up her paring knife as if to suggest she might just try it.

"Perhaps I should bring you with me, as my bodyguard?" Pempasigle said.

"You should do what you always do with your vacation, Pem. Go see your mother and sisters, enjoy three weeks of sleeping in and eating morning mint cookies and complaining about the cost of halahac in the country," Makineng said.

"People who do what they always do end up always doing what they've always done," he said. He did not slap his hand on the cutting block but he laid it there more forcefully than his friend was accustomed to. He resisted the urge to apologize when Makineng flinched.

"Aren't you happy here?" she asked.

I'm happy with you, he did not say and added that to the list of things he had not and could not tell his friend. Not yet.

"Here is … good," he said.

It *was* good. Pempasigle lived for these rare moments when

it was only him and Makineng alone with the sound of their knives against the wood cutting blocks. *Thock-thock, thock-thock,* like hearts beating.

"But I want more," he said. "I want to be a kuchiner."

"You are."

"A *real* kuchiner. A grand kuchiner. I want to train under the masters, learn how to make the dishes they serve in the Kaibig and the Sun Palace, create my own dishes, open a kuchineria of my own one day. You could be my first knife. Imagine that."

"You can do all that without throwing away your hard-earned savings on a myth! The Margin is full of thieves and mercenaries; you're going to end up bleeding in the gutter," Makineng said.

"Vessel of Tears is not a myth." How desperately he wanted to tell her how he came by this information, but an oath was an oath.

"Even if it was real, which it is most certainly not, it would be of the Forsaken. It would be unclean."

"We eat potatoes. Potatoes grow in dirt."

"*Our* dirt."

"Clean dirt?"

"Do not mock me, Pempasigle. The Forsaken were cast out by the patrons. They eat their own young, everyone knows that. They run naked, like animals." The red in Makineng's cheeks could have been anger, but Pempasigle suspected it was embarrassment. "You can make a perfectly fine entry from the ingredients in our own market."

"I don't want a 'perfectly fine entry'. I want to make something memorable. Something none of the judges have tasted before."

The argument continued back and forth until the first knife arrived with the day's menu and scolded Pempasigle for not prepping his station. He rushed to finish sharpening the knives and scrubbing the wood blocks with salt and lemon, but he snuck looks to Makineng all day.

She resolutely avoided his eyes and was not there to see him off at the train station the next morning. He wondered if he had made a mistake, if she might not forgive him this time, until he reached into his coat pocket and found three morning mint cookies wrapped in brown paper.

On the outside of the paper, written in Makineng's beautiful, sweeping scroll, was this: *There is no more memorable flavour than home.*

In the time it had taken Pempasigle to extract himself from the mud and limp after the Prang, she had wandered into a cook shack. The cook shack smelled more of compost than cuisine. By the time he forced down bodily complaints and worked up the courage to step inside, she had eaten half a plate of fat insects and was on a second mug of something green.

Of course she had taken a table at the farthest corner of the room, making his crossing a public spectacle and his bedraggled appearance the subject of unfriendly comments and snickers.

He pointed to the single unoccupied chair across from the Prang. "Do you mind if—"

She kicked the chair. Hard. He yelped as it bounced off his knee and tumbled to a stop several feet away. The Prang snatched one of the insects from the plate and scraped the meat from its belly with a thick yellow fingernail.

All the while, Makineng's voice chittered in his head. *What are you thinking? Was it not enough to lose your savings? To have those men beat and humiliate you? Go to your room, grab your things, and catch the next train out of here!*

No. He had not come this far to give up.

He spread his hands. "Won't you at least——"

"No," the Prang said.

"But I can——"

"No."

"Please."

She sucked meat and juice off the end of her finger and then took a swig of the green liquid. Apparently no other answer was forthcoming.

"I can make you rich." He spat out the words as quickly as his mouth would allow, before she could cut him off.

She lowered the mug and met his eyes for the first time. At last, he had her attention. Her gaze moved from head to toe, and then toe to head. Leaning back in the chair, she crossed her arms over her broad chest.

Pempasigle smiled hopefully.

Then, she laughed. He started to laugh along with her. Her chest shook, and she pounded her fist on the table as the volume and intensity of her laugh swelled. Her whole body shuddered now, and he thought he saw tears in the corners of her eyes. When she started gasping for breath, he seized the moment to retrieve the fallen chair and pull up to the table before she could boot it away again.

"I have a plan," he said.

Her mirth was not finished, however. Guffaws subsided to chuckles but then flared up again until the Prang wiped at her eyes.

"If you can help me, I'll——"

A hand as thick as a slab of prime steak and as leathery as bushmeat slapped down on Pempasigle's hand and pinned it to the table. Try as he might, he could not pull free of the grip.

The Prang's laughter ceased and she leaned forward with a face full of menace.

"Why are you so stupid?" she asked.

A hundred responses leapt to his defence. Mouth open, he looked into the Prang's face. He wondered how old she was. Lines cut into her muddy brown skin reminded him of the deep ravines he had seen on a three-dimensional map in the Sagana Museum. The strength in her hand, however, spoke of youth and vitality. But it was what he saw in her eyes that called back the words perched on the edge of his tongue.

"Why are you so sad?" he asked.

The pause was long enough for him to question if what he had seen was true, but then she flung his hand to one side with a snort of air through her nose. The effect — with those horns pointing toward him — was very much of an ox deciding whether to charge.

"I'm stupid, naïve, careless, whatever you want to call me," Pempasigle said. "You're right. But I have a gift, and it must be honoured. I don't know if your … kind value honour, but —"

"What gift?"

Was anyone allowed to complete a sentence with this Prang, or was it to him alone she devoted her power of interruption?

"I can show you," he said.

The fraction of an incline of the Prang's head he interpreted as permission. He reached for her hand. Before his fingers made contact, she yanked it away. He assured her he would not hurt her and the expression he received in return made him shrink in his skin. He was almost half her height, and his muscles were like a baby's compared to hers.

The Prang is right. You are stupid.

Perhaps she read his mind. Whatever it was, she relented and let him take her hand in his. He raised the hand to his mouth, pressed the backs of the fingers to his nose and inhaled. The stench of the meal overpowered everything else.

"This is the easy part," he said. "I don't know what you call these insects, and some of the spices are unfamiliar, but they were soaked in vinegar and smoked sugar. At least a few hours, I'd say. Fried in some kind of animal fat. The fat is almost rancid and the cooking temperature is too high. The cook is obviously ..."

She did not interrupt him with words this time, but the look on her face conveyed her complete lack of interest.

"Right," Pempasigle said. A smile flickered on and off his face. Now or never. He darted his head forward, took the Prang's index finger into his mouth, and sucked.

The next sensation was a hot, stinging slap across his jaw, which seemed to come apart from his face and then re-attach. The Prang was growling what he assumed were curses in whatever language her people spoke.

"You've been working with some kind of oil," he said. Quickly. Before she could hit him again, or leave. He waggled his jaw from side to side. Talking was going to be painful. "Oil and metal. And there's something else I taste." He folded in his lips and closed his eyes. "You were cleaning a weapon earlier. A weapon and—" He frowned. "Your ears. You haven't eaten much today. Some kind of generic protein ration bar is my best guess, they all taste alike. There's a medicinal flavour, an ointment perhaps. You've been tending a wound? There's another medicine. No, not quite medicine but ..."

The origin of the taste made him pause.

"Yeah?" the Prang asked, when the pause stretched noticeably long. Not asked — *dared.*

"It's not important," he said.

In the dim room, he could only hope that the flush in his cheeks did not show. Makineng was in his head again. *A push addict? A Prang? This is who you choose to trust?*

"I'm a high taster," he said, to break the suddenly awkward silence. "My mother recognized it when I was small and taught me how to use it in cooking. It's a gift. Maybe only one in every ten thousand people has it. My family wasn't wealthy enough to send me to a proper school, but I worked hard and got a position at one of the great houses in Sagana. My dream is to study under the masters."

"You're a cook," the Prang said.

"A kuchiner, technically. I'm only second knife, but —"

"You're a cook. And you want to be a more important cook?"

"It's more complicated than that. You see —" He met her eyes again and saw the impatience building. He was losing his last chance. "Yes. A more important cook. The *most* important cook. But I need to make a special dish first, and the main ingredient is on the other side of the Margin."

Now her interest returned, though what she thought of his plan was impossible to discern. If only emotions were as identifiable as spices.

"And I need someone —"

"I know what you need, City," she said. Her arms were across her chest again. Her chin jutted toward him. "Can't pay for it now, can you?"

"I have a little money left in my room. But, more importantly, I know someone who will buy it. All that I can deliver. I only need one or two for myself, the rest I can sell. Even if we split fifty-fifty, it would be a fortune!"

She didn't push her chair away from the table; she pushed the table toward Pempasigle, caging him in his chair.

"Sixty-forty," he amended.

She stood. The highest point of her horns nearly brushed the ceiling.

"Eighty-twenty!"

She grunted. It was a disturbing sound.

"You can have all the profit. I swear. Only, please help me," he said.

Once more, those boots moved away from him.

His chin dropped to his chest. What a fool he had been.

"Well?"

He spun to see the Prang in the middle of the cook shack. Waiting. She was waiting for him to follow. He sprang out of the chair, forgetting about the table obstructing his exit, and tumbled to the ground. All the injuries from the morning shouted their displeasure, but he ignored the racket.

This time when he limped through the crowd, there was not even a whisper or the smallest titter of laughter.

"I'm Pempasigle Ormutosh," he said, once they were outside. He extended his hand. It hung there, a wallflower at the dance, until his self-consciousness got the better of him and he retracted it.

"Get your things, City," the Prang said.

"You mean, come with you?"

Nothing.

"I think you misunderstood. I can't cross the Margin. I shouldn't even—"

The Prang was heading back into the cook shack.

"Wait!" he called. "I'll come with you."

The Prang stopped.

"I'll just need to get my things." He raised his hands as if to hold her in place. "Don't leave. I'll be quick."

He jogged a few steps then spun around. "I didn't get your name."

"You call me Boss," she said.

"Boss," he said, with a slight upward inflection. There was no question in the Prang's face. "Boss," he repeated, this time as a statement.

And now you are in business with a Prang and travelling into the unclean lands, Makineng chided. *Pray your mother never learns of this.*

At six years old, Pempasigle knew his family kitchen as well as his own mother did and better than either of his sisters. On this day, however, familiarity had vanished as MoMo produced a mystery from the bottom of her worn market basket.

The rough brown cloth had captivated him. MoMo handled the package so gently, Pempasigle wondered if it might contain a newborn child. No, no baby could be that small.

"This is a special treat, just for us," MoMo said.

She laid the package on the wood counter and Pempasigle climbed up on the high stool so that he could see it clearly. His mother's hands, a slightly darker shade of brown than the cloth, paused in their unwrapping.

"Listen to me, Pempasigle Ormutosh," she said. Now he knew this was serious; she only used his full name when she was scolding him or introducing him to someone important. "You are only six, but I believe you are old enough and smart enough to understand that sometimes we must keep secrets. Are you?"

He looked right into his mother's eyes and saw in them a darkness he had never experienced in his young life. Secrets were for fun, whispered between his older sisters or at the back of the temple during long, boring ceremonies. Now he saw — in the eyes he adored — that secrets could be dangerous things. Part of him did not want this new information, but a bigger part of him, the part that knew he was special and different, wanted to take the next step forward into the mysterious lives of adults.

"I am," he said.

She placed one hand on the side of his face and brushed his cheek with her thumb. Before she resumed her work, she approached the house shrine on the windowsill.

Thirteen brief, whispered prayers followed; one prayer for each of the patrons. A prayer to Lakkas for courage. A prayer to Bigayan for a good harvest. A prayer to Payabaan for peace. And so on. Then, she drew the delicate curtains and hid the thirteen figurines from view.

A secret so dark even the patrons could not know of it? Pempasigle shivered both in fear and anticipation.

MoMo returned to her work, peeling back the cloth as carefully as if the contents might shatter at the slightest touch. There was a layer of slick white, almost like a sheet of icing, which she also peeled away. Another layer, underneath that, was some kind of gray sponge, wet, sopping. This spongy layer she had to rip apart with her fingers, though using the same caution she had taken with the layers before.

MoMo pulled the sponge aside, and Pempasigle gasped. Nestled into the sponge was a brilliant violet bulb laced with silver veins, attached to a long white stalk. He had never seen a plant like this, not in the garden, not in the forest, not in the market.

"What is it?" he asked. "Can we eat it?"

"Oh," MoMo said, with a secret-sharing smile, "that is the best part, my little kuchiner."

He reached out to touch it, but his mother grasped his hand and held it firmly.

"This is only for you and me, Pem. I will let you taste it raw, then I will cook it and we will eat it all. But you must never speak of it to anyone, not your father, not your sisters, not even to me — no one. When we are done, we will burn the wrapping and bury the waste."

"Why, MoMo?"

That darkness was back in her eyes. "Because this is the Vessel of Tears, and it is only grown in unclean ground, by the Forsaken."

Pempasigle went cold. The Forsaken were the beasts who lived on the far side of the Margin. Unclean, savage, and cruel: those were the words his father used in front of his children. But Pempasigle had heard more words when his parents did not know he was listening. The Forsaken ate human flesh, they lay with animals, they were little more than animals themselves.

So where had MoMo gotten this forbidden plant, and why would she bring it into their home — a home blessed by all thirteen patrons — in secret?

He was too frightened to ask the question, too frightened now to speak. Perhaps sensing this, his mother rubbed his cheek again.

"Someday, you will be a grand kuchiner, my darling Pem. You will be able to create any flavour you can imagine, and all the richest and most important people in the world will come to taste your dishes. To everyone else this may be blasphemy.

To you ..." The dark serious look returned to her eyes, and Pempasigle was as captive as if she had put him behind bars. "To you, this is education."

She reached for a paring knife and made a shallow cut from the tip of the bulb to its base. Pink liquid seeped out. With the edge of the knife, she folded back the violet skin to expose the pink flesh inside. Next, she cut a small circle of the bulb and nodded for Pempasigle to take it. He did.

The scent reached him long before he raised the piece to his nose. Indescribable to his six-year-old self, the bulb smelled of a hundred different spices at once, it smelled of summer and joy, it smelled of cool nights and clear skies, it smelled of the love he felt for his family and the comfort he felt in their love, it smelled of promise and hope.

He closed his eyes as if in a trance, and he may have been for all he knew. The piece of the bulb touched his tongue, and Pempasigle began to cry because he knew, the way you know that the sun will rise in the morning and set in the evening, that he would never again taste anything so perfect.

"Oh, MoMo," he said, through his tears.

Her arms were around him, her lips on the top of his head.

"I know, I know," she whispered.

The sun was low in the sky. A time of day Pempasigle usually enjoyed. Ordinarily, at sunset, he would be at the staff table, sharing a communal meal, laughing and talking with the rest of the kitchen workers. Makineng would be close, and sometimes their hands or shoulders would touch.

"Shouldn't we start looking for a place to sleep for the evening?" he asked.

The Prang did not reply. As accustomed as he was to taking orders and showing respect to his superiors, Pempasigle was equally used to being shown some modicum of respect in return. At the very least, his questions would be answered.

"I'm not even sure why you need me to come all the way with you. I mean, I can only be a hindrance. You're stronger and faster. You know this road and these lands. I'm as likely to get us lost or killed as anything else," he said. Again. Was this the fourth time he had given this speech or the fifth? He was losing count as well as patience.

He shifted his small pack from the left side to the right and winced. All his injuries were setting in more deeply now. Beneath his clothes he imagined great welts turning dark purple and blue. From what he had seen so far, everything he had been told about Prangs was true. Brutish dullards, this race. A step above the Forsaken in terms of basic civility but lacking the morals and higher sensibilities of humans. Certainly, this one possessed not an ounce of sympathy.

"Aren't you hungry?" he asked. Perhaps an appeal to her baser nature would do the trick. "Because I am starving."

No answer. The Prang — Boss, as she insisted he call her — picked up speed as she trudged up the steep hill, and Pempasigle fought to keep up, lungs burning. She reached the top well ahead of him, stopped and placed both hands on her hips. It almost looked as if she were admiring the view.

Impossible, of course. There was no view in the Margin. Miles and miles of swamp land, that is all there was here. Gnarled trees wrapped in vines and low, scrubby vegetation, all in the same putrid shade of olive green stretched out as far as Pempasigle could see. A single dirt road — human-made — cut through the muck. The hill he climbed now was the only change in elevation Pempasigle had seen all day.

He reached the top, sweating and panting, and stopped beside the Prang. Hands on his knees, he gasped for breath in the choking humidity.

"There," Boss said.

He followed her outstretched finger to a smattering of lights in the distance. Some kind of fort enclosed the road. Whatever it was, the lights marked it as a place where they were likely to find a bed, which Pempasigle imagined falling into without even a morsel of dinner. For once, exhaustion outweighed hunger.

"That's where I'll need you," Boss said.

"For what?" Pempasigle asked.

But she was on the move again, clomping down the hill like an ox headed back to the barn.

In his head, Makineng did not speak. But she laughed. Oh, how she laughed.

Cast in the flickering light of torches and the sickly orange of oil lamps, the inside of the Margin fort looked less like a beacon of welcome than Pempasigle had imagined. Thankfully, no one had questioned their arrival, and less than four steps through the gate they were greeted by a man who, judging by the small contingent of followers waiting silently at his heels, must have held a position of authority.

"There she is! My lovely, my precious Dor! I knew you'd be back."

Pempasigle gaped at the man — dangerous looking in his own right — who was fawning all over his Prang companion. Lovely? Precious? Was he blind?

"Your old room is ready, just how you left it," the man continued, undeterred by Boss's silence. "Well, might have to kick a few bungs out, but that's easily done." He raised a hand, snapped his fingers, and barked out orders to ready Dor's room.

"We're not staying, Brult," Boss said.

This was news to Pempasigle. It was dark. They had been walking all day. Every inch of his body ached. This fort was the only hint of civilization—as loosely as it resembled the word—that he had seen.

"Now, come on, Dor, where else you gonna go?" Brult asked.

As much as the gleam in Brult's eye made him tighten his grip on the straps of the pack that contained the last remnants of his belongings, Pempasigle agreed with the sentiment.

"Not your concern, just need passage for me and him," Boss—or Dor—said. "In and out. Three days. Four at the most."

Brult turned his eyes on Pempasigle for the first time. Makineng's voice in his head was no longer chiding, and there was no laughter. *This is a bad man, Pem. This is the worst kind of man.*

Pempasigle had seen this kind of look before. It was the look his mother had at the market, sizing up the goods, deciding which cut of meat would be most tender. Brult smiled. A gold tooth winked.

"Well, you know the price for passage, Dor," Brult said. The tone of his voice, in the space of a few breaths, had become like the roll of thunder.

At his side, Dor inclined her head. She knew the price. Pempasigle could not say why it bothered him, that tiny gesture of acknowledgement.

"I'll need a push," she said.

"Course you will, darling," Brult purred. "Wouldn't be a show without that."

Pempasigle heard himself speaking and was unable to stop. "Boss, we don't have to —"

"This is City," Dor told Brult. "He's mine."

"Yummy," Brult said.

"No one touches him," Dor said. "Not a finger."

"Wouldn't dream," Brult said. "Why don't you clean up, precious? I'll find your friend a prime seat."

Dor grabbed the strap of Pempasigle's pack and dragged him away a short distance. She slapped a hand over his mouth before he could utter a single word.

"Don't be stupid," she said. "Don't eat anything. Don't drink anything. Don't go anywhere except where Brult sits you."

He nodded against her hand.

For a second it looked as if she would say more, but she simply pulled her hand away and pushed him back toward Brult. Then she was stalking off once more in that way she always did, as if her destination demanded complete focus.

Brult, with none of the friendly showmanship he had used with Dor, called for him to follow. But Pempasigle watched his companion until she disappeared into a shabby tin shack. He licked his lips where her hand had been.

He tasted fear.

Pempasigle had wanted his last day in his family home to be a celebration. Instead, he had found himself frozen, clutching his travel bag, unable to take a single step.

His mother had taken a seat next to him on the edge of his bed. Pempasigle did not fight off the hand that stroked his hair or bristle at the use of the pet name he had long outgrown.

"What's wrong, my little kuchiner? What are you afraid of?" she asked.

"I think I should stay. Here, with you," he said. "Pahlam and Talino are busy with their own families, and you won't have anyone to carry wood for you now that Father's gone. And——"

"What are you afraid of?" she asked again.

He glanced down at the single bag that contained all the belongings he would take to the city to start his new job. His new life.

Inside, wrapped in a leather case, were the knives his parents had saved up to buy him. Beside them were carefully wrapped jars of his favourite spices—some that could only be found here, in the village of his birth. Beside the spices, an envelope. This letter had come three weeks earlier. Pempasigle could recite it by heart. The seal at the bottom made it official. He was now an employee of the kitchen of the Nasa Kipang family.

"What if I'm not good enough?" he asked his mother.

"They would not give you a job if they did not think you were good enough," she said.

"Good enough to sweep floors and wash dishes."

"That is just the start. You have to prove yourself."

"But what if I can't?" He stood and raised a palm toward the window. "Here, I know what I am. Here, I'm special; I'm Pempasigle the little kuchiner, the boy with the gift. There, I will be just another dish pig. How can I hope to compete with those rich city people and their special schools?"

His mother pursed her lips. He waited for the soft words of encouragement, the patient inspiration. Instead, she stood, smoothed her aging hands down the front of her orange smock, and walked to the door of his bedroom.

"MoMo?" he said, feeling very much like a small boy again.

She turned to him and for the first time in his life Pempasigle read disappointment on his mother's face.

"There is nothing more sacred than purpose. Nothing more valuable than opportunity," she said. "You are rich, my son. I wish you could see how rich you are."

In the centre of the dirt ring, a squat man in a raggedy red coat shouted through a dented bullhorn. "Back for one night only, back for bloody revenge, the Beast of Bellador, the Maniac of the Margin, the one and only … Dor the Dreadful!"

The crowd leapt to their feet, shouted, clapped, stomped on the rickety wooden bleachers. In the torchlight, Brult's face was sinister, and Pempasigle strangled the straps of his pack.

"Love her, they do," Brult said, with a glint of gold tooth. His breath stank of decay and stale liquor. When Pempasigle tried to lean away, Brult leaned in closer and nudged him with an elbow. "You're in for a treat tonight, city boy."

Before he could answer, Dor entered the ring. The longcoat was gone. Her chest was bare but for a studded strap of black leather that cinched around her breasts. Her horns were adorned with metal decorations, rings and spikes that jangled as she walked. More black leather wrapped her hands and knees, more studs thrust out from the material. Dor's face was painted to resemble a skull. The combined effect was monstrous.

Long, thudding strides carried her into the middle of the ring to tumultuous applause. Chants of "Dor, Dor, Dor!" echoed. She circled the ring, baring her teeth to the crowd and growling. This incited even more cheers.

"What a beauty," Brult said.

Beauty was not the word that came to Pempasigle's mind, especially when Dor walked by his seat and he saw that her pupils were wide, her gaze unfocused and rabid. Up close, he also saw the multitude of scars that criss-crossed every inch of visible flesh. Breath deserted him; his companion was the living incarnation of his childhood nightmares.

The man in the red coat raised the bullhorn and shouted another long stream of pronouncements. Pempasigle heard only the name — Andlat the Assassin — and noticed another well-decorated Prang enter the ring. He could not take his eyes off Dor. Then he felt that elbow in his ribs again.

"I said, first time with a Prang, hey?" Brult said.

When he tried to answer, Pempasigle's mouth was too dry and all he could do was cough. This triggered a saucy laugh from his leering host.

"Don't worry, city boy, she only turns it on for the show. She'll be gentle as rain with you," Brult said. "'Less you want her rough." He plucked at the sleeve of Pempasigle's bloodstained shirt. "By the looks of it, maybe you do."

There was no time for rebuttal; the man in the red coat was announcing the rules of the match, few as they were. A gong sounded, and the crowd guffawed as the red-coated man scurried to get out of the path of the charging competitors.

Dor ran, head lowered, and drove her horns into those of her opponent. The clash shook the ground, and a sickening thud forced Pempasigle to turn his head. He looked back long enough to see Dor drive her studded fist into the cheek of the 'Assassin'. A spray of blood hit the dirt; the crowd hollered for more.

This time when Pempasigle looked away, he heard Brult chuckling.

The fight became a series of meaty smacks, thuds, cracks,

cheers, and boos. Makineng's running commentary in his head reminded him how sheltered his life had been, how little he knew of the world beyond the kitchen or the market.

When the cheers and boos turned to a more ominous rumble, Pempasigle's eyes were drawn back to the dirt ring. Dor was bloody; many of the decorations on her horns were gone. Her opponent pummelled her with a hurricane of punches to her head and midsection. Feebly, Dor tried to strike back, but her fists slipped off the other Prang. Then the Assassin lunged, wrapped his thick arms around Dor's waist, and tackled her to the ground.

The crowd gasped as one. The two bodies landed. The assassin leaned back and then drove his horns into Dor's head. Her body jolted from the concussion, and then she lay still.

A hand on his arm was the first realization Pempasigle had that he had stood. Brult shook his head and pulled him down. "Sit until the show's over. Patience, now."

Pempasigle wanted to argue the point—Dor was knocked out, what else could there be—but he guessed Brult was not the type to be swayed by logic.

The Assassin climbed off Dor and raised his hands skyward. Those who had cheered so loudly for Dor quickly switched allegiances and cheered for her opponent. Not content with the applause, or the victory, the Assassin grabbed one of Dor's horns and dragged her through the dirt, around the circle, showing off his prize. This elicited the response he was looking for. On their feet, the crowd stomped and howled.

Brult signalled a woman and a man hovering nearby, and they began to move through the audience, collecting bills. Wagers, Pempasigle assumed.

The Assassin had dropped Dor's prone body back to the dirt and was headed out of the ring. Pempasigle stood again.

"Easy," Brult said. "Your sweetheart is fine. We'll clean her up and have you on your way soon enough. Sit."

Though he did so reluctantly, resentfully, Pempasigle followed his instructions. Two men carried Dor away. There was nothing he could do — for her or himself — right now. He did not dare consider that she might not wake up. That he might be stuck here, alone.

"Savages," he muttered.

Brult laughed again. "Oh, I do love you civilized folk and your short memories." He pulled something from his pocket and stuffed it in the corner of his mouth, which Pempasigle could now see was missing a variety of teeth. What teeth remained were stained and chipped.

"You made her do that," Pempasigle said. "Didn't you?"

"Cost of passage. Dor knows it," Brult said. "She must really fancy you, city boy. Last time I saw her, she told me she was never coming back. And here she is."

The crowd was thinning, shuffling out of the wooden stands and off to the ramshackle tin shacks that promised more sick pleasures. Pempasigle craned his neck, searching for a sign of Dor.

"Never said why she's taking you into the swamp," Brult continued. "You looking for some taboo? Forsaken flesh? Just once. No one back home has to know, hey?"

The man's lurid wink made Pempasigle gag. "That's foul."

Brult shrugged. "Hardly stops you civilized types from trying it. Unclean, my ass. Anyway, not like you haven't done worse to 'em." He spit a stream of dark green mulch to one side, and some of it splashed up on his trousers. "But you go home and say your pretty words to those fourteen patrons, and all is forgiven."

"Thirteen," Pempasigle said. "There are thirteen patrons."

"Fourteen." Brult stood and nodded to the left where Dor was limping out of a low doorway. "Here comes one now. Happy travels."

Alone in the stands, Pempasigle turned the strange conversation over in his head. Dor's coat was back on, the decorations were gone. Just a regular Prang once more. Whatever that meant.

He hurried over to her, just in time to catch her as she stumbled. His legs buckled under her weight. It took a few tottering steps before he figured out how to balance her bulk.

"Where are we going?" he asked.

She raised a hand and pointed.

"This is why you needed me, isn't it?" he asked.

"Gotta get out of here," she slurred.

Pempasigle shifted her weight again and then began the long, precarious march to the exit gates. He gazed out over the dismal encampment and the empty dirt ring.

"Yes, this is no place for us," he said.

Tell me what you're going to do with it," Dor said.

"The Vessel of Tears?" Pempasigle asked. She nodded and he tried, once more, to find a comfortable position on the hard wooden floor of the shack she had led them to for the night. "I'm going to cook with it."

Her laughter was eerie. The push she had taken before her fight back at the fort lingered in her system. "I *know* you're going to cook with it," she half-slurred. "I mean, why's it so important?"

He considered not telling her. The sun had been down for hours, his stomach growled, and his head ached. All he wanted was sleep. But between the distant screeches in the swamp and the lack of a bed, sleep had become an impossible fantasy. Besides, he had witnessed the price of their passage; he owed her.

"There's a school in the city where I live. The Grand Sagalan Kuchiner Academy. All the greatest kuchiners train there. The tuition is high … higher than I could ever hope to pay. But once a year they hold a competition. Anyone can enter. One dish—that is all you are allowed to make. Thousands compete, but the school only awards three scholarships. To win, you can't just be good; you must be unique, memorable. Some dishes don't even get tasted; the judges can tell just from the presentation that they are not good enough. Most only get a single bite before they are discarded. The judges must taste in your dish the promise of a Grand Kuchiner: complete dedication to the art."

There were only filaments of moonlight inside the shack, but Pempasigle's eyes had adjusted. Dor gazed at him like a child listening to a bedtime tale of magic.

"Food is art?" she said.

"It can be," Pempasigle said. "Fried bugs and protein bars can sustain our bodies, but only art can nourish our hearts and souls. Braised leg of tantaurine in halahac jelly. Spun sugar snowflake towers drizzled in brierberry-infused chocolate. Beet and pear nopolini with rose ginger juice. These are dishes that dance on the tongue, that paint pictures and conjure up memories. These dishes are art."

Dor's mouth hung open. A Prang enchanted.

"You think you can win?" she asked.

"With the Vessel of Tears, I'm sure I can."

"Why?"

"It's—have you never tasted it?" he asked.

Dor shook her head. "What does it taste like?"

"Like love," Pempasigle said. His lips slid into a smile at the memory. "Like all the happiest moments of your life squeezed together and then bursting open all at once."

"Sounds nice." Dor's eyes glazed over once more. Pempasigle wondered if it was the drugs, or if all those ramming blows to the head might have addled her brain.

"Your friend Brult said something strange to me. He said there were fourteen patrons," Pempasigle said.

"He was teasing you."

Something in Dor's face, a shadow of sadness, made him question the truth of that. But he let it drop, since it seemed to make her uncomfortable.

For several minutes, they lay in the dark, listening to the creatures that haunted the swamp outside. At length, Pempasigle cleared his throat and said the words that had been buzzing around his head since they had left the fort.

"If I'd known the price of passage, I'd never have asked for you to come here."

"I know," Dor said.

Then, thinking about another of Brult's comments: "Do others from the city come here? To where the Forsaken live?"

Dor rolled until her back was to him. "Not with me." He was about to offer an apology when she said, "Tell me about your home."

"My home is—" He was about to describe the city to her, but something stopped him. Home. He lived in the city, but his home would always be in his family's village. "It's peaceful. In the morning, I walk to the market. On the way, I pick fresh herbs along the river bank—water trumpet, peppergrass, rose ginger."

He carried on with the description until he heard her breathing become deep, eventually changing to snores.

"Goodnight, Dor," he whispered, and closed his eyes.

The late afternoon sun prickled Pempasigle's skin as he walked in Dor's lengthening shadow. On this side of the fort, the path was overgrown and often too narrow to walk side by side — even if he had been able to keep up with the Prang's punishing pace.

Don't scratch. Don't scratch. Don't scratch. As much as Pempasigle repeated the words, he could not stop his fingers from raking at the insect bites that covered most of his body.

"I still don't know why we couldn't have slept back at the fort," he told Dor.

She did not answer, not even a grunt. The drug had worn off and she was back to her usual non-conversational self. Six hours of walking and she had spoken ten words — Pempasigle had counted.

"Is it much farther? If you had warned me, I would have packed some food. And water. I didn't think —"

Dor stopped, raised her hands to either side of her mouth, and let out a long screech.

Had he angered her? Was Dor the Dreadful going to turn and charge him now?

And then he heard it, a similar screech but from a distance.

"Is that the Forsaken?" Pempasigle asked. He scratched more furiously now, nerves adding to the general discomfort.

"Stay behind me," Dor said, and walked on.

Despite his empty stomach, Pempasigle felt a sudden urge to empty his bowels. *Don't let them touch you*, Makineng warned.

He followed behind Dor as instructed but did not allow

more than a few paces between them. The only nearby hiding places were off the single road, in the swamp. And who knew what lived in that muck.

A shape appeared on the horizon. It was joined by more shapes. From his place behind Dor, Pempasigle could see them climbing out of what looked like unusual trees and scampering across wooden platforms to the road. Closer still and he could hear them talking—high pitched squeaks and clicks—and could see that the 'trees' were actually thatch houses built on taller platforms, like nests.

Their size surprised him. Everything he knew about the Forsaken came from stories. In his mind they had been giant razor-toothed monsters. Here, in front of him, the tallest stood no higher than his chest. The children barely reached the top of Dor's boots. They looked as if they were made of clay. Their mostly naked bodies were dark gray, covered in smooth hair, with wide saucer eyes that were dark from rim to rim. They did have sharp teeth, but they were smiling.

They were smiling at Dor.

"Stay here," Dor said, and she crossed the remaining ten feet between them and the Forsaken.

Pempasigle scratched and stared. The group—about twenty-five was his guess—surrounded the towering Prang. They ran their hands over her legs and arms, chittering at her all the while. The children climbed up on her feet or grabbed her long coat and swung from it. She bowed, and one of the older children scrambled up onto her head, clutching the horns for support when Dor straightened.

Most surprising of all, Dor—whose voice was deep and throaty—spoke to the Forsaken in that same high-pitched squeak.

She pointed toward him, and Pempasigle froze mid-scratch as all the Forsaken turned their saucer eyes on him. The chittering quieted to whispers. They seemed to be sizing him up. Judging. Why? If a Prang was no threat, how could they have any worry about him?

After more chittering between Dor and the group, two of the Forsaken started toward Pempasigle. They pointed at his face, still talking between themselves. It was difficult to read their expressions, but they seemed concerned. It was also difficult to tell them apart or to guess at their gender even though their clothing consisted of only a strip of cloth that hung from their waist in the front and back.

The one was who was slightly taller stopped right in front of Pempasigle and waved his hand up and down.

"Bow," Dor called. "Bend forward."

He nodded, swallowed, and bent forward at the waist. The Forsaken leaned in, grabbed Pempasigle's face and then licked him across the forehead.

"Hey!" Pempasigle pushed the creature away and jumped back.

This triggered angry chittering between the two Forsaken in front of him. Dor strode forward, the children still clutching her coat and horns, swinging like decorations. She spoke to the pair. Heads nodded. One of the children hopped off Dor's coat and sprinted off the road and into the swamp.

"They shouldn't have done …" Pempasigle stuttered. "I mean, you shouldn't touch someone like that."

"Shut up, City," Dor said.

The child returned, skin dripping, hands clutching clumps of weeds. The Forsaken who had licked Pempasigle took some of the weeds, stuffed them in his mouth, and chewed rapidly.

He spit the pulpy green mush into the outstretched hands of his companion, who offered them up to Pempasigle.

"I'm not supposed to eat that, am I?" he asked Dor.

The Forsaken clicked and chirped at him.

"Rub it on your bites," Dor said.

With a grimace, Pempasigle scooped some of the mush onto his fingers. He didn't dare put it on his face, but he was acutely aware that to turn down this 'gift' might be a grave insult. The Forsaken were small, but there were a lot of them, and they did have sharp teeth.

He dabbed some of the pulp onto his blistered and red forearm. Immediately, the fiery skin cooled. In the spot the pulp covered, the itch vanished. He raised his arm to his nose and sniffed—the scent was unfamiliar.

The Forsaken laughed. The sound reminded him of birds.

"Can I have more?" he asked, but the Forsaken were already gathering and chewing more of the miracle weeds.

"You could have warned me," he told Dor.

"Sure," she said.

It may have been a trick of the late afternoon light, but he was almost certain he had seen her smile.

The boat, if it could be called that, creaked and threatened to topple. At first, Dor's presence had been a welcome relief—as helpful as the Forsaken had been so far, Pempasigle had not relished the idea of paddling out into the swamp with them on his own—but now Dor's weight, in the deeper water, was a liability.

Long shadows were swallowed by the approaching night and the thickness of the vegetation. Pempasigle heard only the dip of the oars and the beating of his heart. Every now and then he swore he felt something nudge the unsteady wooden skiff. Something lurking below.

The two Forsaken chittered softly. Sombrely?

A clump of tall reeds scraped the side of the boat and the paddling slowed. One of the paddlers spoke. Dor replied.

"Are we there?" Pempasigle asked.

"Close," she answered, quietly.

More soft chittering.

"You need to be quiet. Don't move," Dor said.

The taller of the two Forsaken grasped a reed, pulled the boat in close, and brought it to a stop. The other pointed to a circle of water surrounded by the tall plants. Squinting into the darkness, Pempasigle saw nothing. Then, as his eyes adjusted, he made out shapes about six inches below the surface. Bulbous, white, shifting with the movement of the water and attached by a long stem.

"Vessel of Tears," Pempasigle whispered.

He counted eight. Eight bulbs, each of which possessed the potential to change his life forever. Even Dor appeared interested, though she was careful not to shift her weight and risk unbalancing the boat as she peered into the water.

Chittering.

"They can give you four," Dor said.

He calculated. He would need at least one to practice. One for the actual dish. That left two to sell. Would two be enough to pay Dor for her services? They had not even discussed what that cost would be. The bulbs varied in size, too. Which would be more valuable — bigger or smaller? He had never thought to ask. Perhaps two of each would be best. Big and small.

"Four will do. But can you tell them which ones I would like?"

he asked Dor. Then he pointed to two of the smaller bulbs, one of the bigger bulbs, and one bulb that was easily four times the size of the rest.

The hushed chittering between the two forsaken intensified and there was a lot of twitching and hand flapping.

"You can't have that one," Dor said. She pointed to the largest bulb.

"Why not?" Pempasigle said.

Dor bent forward from the waist and pinned her gaze on him. "Because you can't."

He swallowed and shrank back from her. "That one, then?" He pointed to the next largest bulb.

Dor spoke to the Forsaken and then nodded to Pempasigle.

The Forsaken holding the boat in place wrapped a thin rope around the reeds. It — Pempasigle had come to think of them as 'it' since he could not confidently say he or she — broke the top off of one of the reeds and rubbed it between its hands vigorously. When it pulled its hands apart, a dull glow shone from them. The hands, held up over the water, acted as a dim lantern. By that light, the other Forsaken bent over the side of the boat and dipped its arms in the water.

The time required to harvest each bulb was excruciating. It seemed that the length of the stalk, where it was severed, was critical. Great care was also taken once the plant was plucked. Glowing Hands would hold the delicate prize while its companion dunked completely under the water to retrieve more vegetation from the bottom. Pempasigle recognized this as the gray spongy layer he had seen his mother's bulb wrapped in. The sponge was laid on the floor of the boat and the bulb placed gently on top. This was repeated for all four bulbs.

When all were collected, Glowing Hands lit the bulbs while Gardener—as Pempasigle had come to think of the other Forsaken—used its fingers to pry open the very tip of each plant. The new opening resembled a flower, something Pempasigle did not remember from his mother's bulb. With all four bulbs opened that way, Gardener raised its wrist to Glowing Hands's mouth. They chittered softly and then Glowing Hands bit down on the wrist.

Pempasigle gasped and backed away from the pair, though that only meant a few more inches of distance given the confines of the boat.

He watched, horrified, as Gardener moved its wrist over the first bulb and let several drops of blood fall into the open flower.

"It … they shouldn't do that!" Pempasigle said. "They're ruining them. Why is—"

He felt rather than saw Dor's look of caution and disapproval and went silent. Inside, his guts churned. Is that what they had done with his mother's bulb? Had he and his beloved MoMo eaten Forsaken blood? Had he and his mother always been unclean?

The drops fell until the flower-opening closed, and Gardener moved onto the next bulb. All four sealed, Gardener pressed a broad leaf against its wrist and chittered to Glowing Hands. Together the two wrapped the bulbs in the sponge, which also sealed itself around each package.

Once all the bulbs were protected by the sponge, the two Forsaken scooped several buckets of water over them.

Glowing Hands untied the bow line from the reeds, and Gardener leaned over into the water one more time. It rubbed its hands on the outside of that giant bulb and chittered in a soothing sing-song voice before they pushed off. The Forsaken took care to push the wall of reeds back into place to hide their watery garden patch.

They rode back in complete darkness, which did not impede the paddlers' speed. And though he could not see the bulbs, Pempasigle stared at where he knew they lay, safe in their wrapping.

His prized ingredient, his glorious hope, was contaminated. If he used even a piece of these bulbs in his entry for the competition, he would be responsible for making each of the judges unclean and condemning them to an eternity apart from all their loved ones after death. An eternity of heartache and suffering.

You cannot, Makineng warned. *No prize is worth another's soul.*

The thatch nest was more comfortable than the wooden shack from the night before but less roomy. Pempasigle struggled to find a position that would allow him to sleep without touching the Prang next to him, with no success. Not that sleep would come anytime soon. His tainted bundle was tucked inside his pack, silently taunting him.

"Stop moving," Dor growled.

"You're enjoying this, aren't you?" he snapped in return. "You wanted me to see that. You wanted me to know that I've wasted all my time and money and hard work on … on … filth."

No answer from Dor. Of course.

"I actually thought you wanted to help me. I'm stupid, just like you said."

Silence.

"Well, go ahead, laugh. I fell for it. I've got four plants that might as well be poison and barely enough money to get home. Oh, and I've also learned that I am unclean. How can I possibly ever dream of asking —" He choked on her name. "You've killed all my dreams. Everything they told me about Prangs was true."

Nothing.

"What do you care, right? Doing push and fighting, that's all you Prangs dream about. What would you know about wanting something better, something pure?"

Still nothing.

"I guess I'll just sell them all now. And don't worry, you'll get your share. I'd hate to keep you out of drug money. I may be stupid, but I keep my promises."

"It's not a plant," Dor said.

"Is that supposed to make me feel better?" Pempasigle asked.

"You couldn't have the biggest one because it's been fertilized. It holds a life."

Pempasigle's rage subsided enough for him to consider these words.

"You mean …" He shook his head in the dark. "The Vessel of Tears are their children?" Bile rose.

"Their eggs," Dor said.

"I feel sick."

"You eat bird eggs, don't you?" Dor asked.

"That's different."

"How?"

"They're … It's … Birds don't talk and have communities and —"

"Maybe they do, but you never noticed because you think they're just dumb animals," Dor said.

"That's ridiculous," Pempasigle said. Even so, fingers of doubt poked him. "So they're eggs. That doesn't make them any less unclean. It makes them more unclean. It was bad enough with the blood. Now you're telling me these plants actually come *out* of the Forsaken?"

"That's not their name," Dor said.

"I don't care."

"I know."

"Then why even say it?"

"Someone should," Dor said.

"You make no sense."

"Where do you come from?"

"You know where I come from. I told you I grew up in —"

"Where did your people come from? All of your people. From the beginning."

Pempasigle frowned in the dark. "You mean the settlers and the thirteen patrons?"

"Them," Dor said.

"Everyone knows that. The story of our journey has been told for thousands of years. What does that —"

"Where did the *C'tkitet*, your 'Forsaken' come from?" Dor asked.

Pempasigle dug into his memories of temple sermons and stories told by his family and friends. Much had been said of the evil nature of the Forsaken, of their animal tendencies, of their depraved behaviour but nothing that he could recall of their origins.

"I don't know,' he admitted.

"You'd be surprised how much you don't know," Dor said.

"Where did they come from?"

"Nowhere," Dor said.

"How —"

"They were here when the settlers arrived. This is their world, City. Was their world."

"But the Book of Days says the settlers were sent to pure worlds, for their safety. Only plants and trees and beasts could inhabit the chosen world. If the For—if these creatures were here before us, then …"

"Then you call them beasts so you can slaughter them with a clear conscience."

"That's not true," Pempasigle said.

"Then what is the truth?" Dor asked.

Pempasigle rolled the question around and around in his head. Until today, he had never seen a Forsaken in the flesh. He knew they existed, in small numbers, in the lands beyond the Margin. Now he could not stop the questions from coming. Had their numbers always been small? Had they always lived only beyond the Margin? What had happened the when the settlers arrived on this planet that was supposedly chosen for its lack of other intelligent life—a farm and garden for the settlers to develop and cultivate?

He tried and could not imagine his people, with all their knowledge and love of beauty and art, their devotion to peace and cooperation, killing off or driving out a population of likewise sentient beings. However strange they appeared, these creatures were not beasts, even he had to admit that. They had language, they had clothing (sparse as it was), they had tools and medicine, they even had art, at least in the form of singing. They had treated him, a stranger, kindly. They had not even accepted the small sum of money he had offered for the bulbs (the eggs, he knew now), but had taken only some samples of the spice he carried with him.

These were people not beasts, by any description, and yet surely the Forsaken had not come here with the settlers. Either Dor was lying or …

"Who slaughtered them?" he asked.

Silence.

"Dor?"

"Go to sleep, City."

The fort that had held such allure on that first day seemed shabby now. Pempasigle noticed, for the first time, that armed guards — Prang and human — stood watch from the towers overhead and at the entry gates. Who was there to keep out aside from the Forsaken?

Dor walked at Pempasigle's side, though he no longer felt in need of her protection. The inhabitants of this Margin outpost were more pitiable than frightening. Some sprawled in the bleachers surrounding the ring where Dor had fought, sleeping off too much push or liquor or who knew what other intoxicant from the night before.

Livestock bleated and snorted in makeshift pens. Women in stained and torn skirts dumped dishwater into the dirt street. Children ran barefoot with sticks tied to their heads to mimic Prang horns. They snorted and played at wrestling.

Pempasigle's pack was heavy, but he dared not pass it off or set it down. He still wasn't certain what he would do with the contents, but he recognized that he had been given something far more precious than a mere plant. These were eggs. The possibility of children for a race driven to the edge of extinction.

As they had the day before, Pempasigle and Dor walked without speaking.

"There's my beauty!" Brult's voice broke the heavy silence between them.

Dor only nodded at the man. Pempasigle saw, in the light

of day, that Brult had a distinct hobble to his step. An injury? A deformity?

"Get what you came for?" Brult asked him, with that lewd wink.

"More," Pempasigle said.

"Glad to hear it! Another satisfied customer. Make sure to tell all your friends back home in the uppity up-up now, won't you?" Brult said.

Pempasigle did not respond and Dor did not stop. They both walked on toward the gate on the other side — the gate out of this sad place. Brult hobble-stepped to keep up.

"Don't you be a stranger, Dor, my lethal lovely," Brult cooed. "Everyone's been talking 'bout your performance. Figure we should let you win the next one, hey?"

Let? Pempasigle's muscles tightened.

"Go away, Brult," Dor said.

"As you wish, my sweet. But you know where to find me. You always know where to find old Brult!" he said and grinned.

Then he was gone, and the silence descended again until they reached the exit gate.

"You know the way from here," Dor said.

"You're not coming?" Pempasigle asked.

No answer. As usual.

"I'll send you the money as soon as I sell the —" He had almost said plants. "As soon as I sell them. Just tell me where to send it. Can I send a credit note or do you need —"

"Just go, City. Go win your prize."

"I promised you I'd split the earnings and I meant it. I owe you."

Dor stepped close and gazed down on him. In her eyes, he saw that same sadness he had caught back in the cook shack.

"You don't have to keep doing this, Dor. You can come with me. You can …" His voice trailed away. What could she be outside of this place? What would she be in the city but a freak and an outcast?

After a lengthy pause, he asked, "Where did you come from? Where did the Prangs come from?"

She smiled. It was the most heartbreaking thing he had ever seen.

Silence.

"You helped those"—he could not remember or pronounce the name Dor had used—"people somehow, didn't you?"

"Sometimes people need help," she said.

"Why did you help me?" Pempasigle asked.

Dor looked away, directly into the rising sun. He expected another round of silence.

"I wanted to be part of something beautiful. Just once," she said.

Pempasigle's throat tightened. He opened his mouth to speak, but she was already walking away from him.

He watched her stride back toward Brult, watched the man lead her off to that dirty tin shack. He knew what would happen—tonight, and the next night, and the next.

He let her go.

On his first vacation break, Pempasigle had practically run to the train station, eager to return to his family, to the comfort of his home, to share the news of his new job and the amazing sights in the city. This time he had dragged his heels, finding excuses to pop into the kitchen and catch one last glimpse of Makineng, and had almost missed his train.

"Tell me about this girl?" his mother had asked.

She rubbed some salt between her fingers and let it drop into the soup. Pempasigle leaned in to sniff the bubbling broth and received a smack on the hand.

"Away! I taught you this recipe. You wouldn't let me stick my nose into your cooking, now, would you?" she said.

"You mean like you do every time I cook here, MoMo?" Pempasigle teased.

"Pssh, you always did have an imagination. Now, no more stalling. I want to know about this Makineng you talk about the same way you used to talk about your favourite cakes."

"I told you, we work in the kitchen together. She comes from a good family—a very good family—and we're friends, that's all," he said.

"You are a terrible liar, my little kuchiner," MoMo said. She dipped the spoon into the broth, blew on it and then sipped. She held the spoon out to Pempasigle, who also sipped. "More ginger?"

"More ginger," he agreed.

"Have you met her family?" his mother asked.

"Of course not. How could I? What do I have to offer? I'm not even first knife yet."

"What does that matter?"

"It matters. In the city, these things matter—your family name, your job title, how much money you earn."

"Have you asked Makineng if those things matter to her?" His mother poured out two small bowls and passed one to Pempasigle.

He took a spoonful and closed his eyes, smiling. No matter how many dishes he learned to make, no matter how exotic the ingredients, it was always his mother's food that most delighted his senses.

"Well?" MoMo asked.

"Why would I ask her that? If it matters to everyone else, it matters to her, and it certainly matters to her family. If I am accepted in the academy, *after* I graduate, when I am worthy of her, I will tell her of my feelings and ask to meet her family."

"My boy." MoMo laid her spoon beside her bowl and placed her hand—even more aged than the last visit home—over his hand. "You see this soup. There is nothing special about it. No secret ingredients, no fancy spices, no complicated cooking technique. It is a very plain soup. Surely you've had much better in your new home. And yet every time you come here it is the first thing you ask me to make. Why is that?"

"Because it reminds me of home. Because it may be a simple recipe, but you are the only one who can make it taste like this."

She squeezed his hand. "Would this soup taste any better served in a fancy kuchineria, in crystal bowls with golden spoons?"

"Of course not. But—"

"You will be 'worthy' of her when you know your own mind, when you act on your own convictions and not on the notions of others." She smiled, and all the wrinkles that made his mother so beautiful sprang into place. "Now, eat your soup before it gets cold!"

The inside of the tin shack where Pempasigle had found Dor was just as filthy and dark as he had imagined on that first foray into the Margin fort, less than a week before. There was a single straw mattress in one corner, but Dor showed no interest in moving there, and carrying her was out of the question. He knelt at her side, steaming bowl in one hand, spoon in the other.

"You have to eat it before it gets cold," Pempasigle said. "Come on, sit up, you can do it."

Dor grunted and lifted her head a fraction.

"Too tired," she said, and slumped back down to the floor.

Pempasigle sighed and placed bowl and spoon carefully on the floor. He slid his coat off and bundled it up, then lifted Dor's enormous head and pushed the 'pillow' underneath. He used one of his handkerchiefs to wipe off the blood that continued to leak from the cut over her right eye.

Both eyes were bloodshot, the pupils still dilated from the push she must have taken before the fight. According to what he had heard, it was a fight she had won, for all the difference it made. How much longer could she go on like this?

You know the answer, Makineng said.

"Why're you here?" she slurred. Her eyes continued their effort to focus on him.

"I brought you dinner," he said, and raised the steaming bowl to show her.

"Not hungry," she said.

"You will be once you taste this. Now open your mouth."

After a brief grumble, she opened her mouth. The drug, at least, made her compliant.

Pempasigle lifted the spoon to his own mouth, blew on it, and then gently poured the broth into Dor's mouth. Her lips came together. She closed her eyes. She stayed like that long enough that he began to wonder if she had passed out.

Then, a tear.

A single tear rolled out of Dor's eye. Its track zigged and zagged as it ran into her many scars and wrinkles.

"No," she said.

"Open," he said. She opened her mouth once more, and Pempasigle gave her another spoonful.

When she opened her eyes, they were watery and not, he knew, from the drug.

"You're wasting it," she said.

"I have three left. More than enough for what I need." He gave her another spoonful and was thrilled to see some life return to her battered face.

One last lie. She would find the note he had tucked into her coat tomorrow, after she had straightened out, after he was long gone. What she did with the credit from the sale of the other three eggs would be her choice, even if that choice was to leave it unclaimed.

He dipped the spoon into the bowl once more.

"Where did the Prangs come from, Dor?" He spoke gently, in the way his mother might have done.

The heartbreaking smile rose, then fell.

"You made us," she said. "To protect you."

Her explanation triggered no surprise. Something about it felt instantly true, right down into his bones.

It made sense. He had seen a piece of the world beyond the carefully constructed cities and villages. He had glimpsed how wild this planet must have been once. There must have been a time when the Prangs had been necessary, as vital to the settlers as the temples and markets and art galleries now were to their descendants. And when the land had been tamed, their 'enemies' vanquished, the settlers made safe and the cities civilized, what then?

He raised the spoon to her lips.

"Why?" she asked.

In the ruddy light of the tin shack, he looked at the broken Prang, the warrior abandoned by a population that no longer needed her gifts.

Another spoonful. A smile. No one in the city would ever appreciate this dish as much as Dor did right now. He wiped away the blood once more and stroked a hand across her cheek.

"Because you deserve to be part of something beautiful."

Makineng burst into the house shrine, her long hair loose and bouncing as she moved. In the weeks since Pempasigle had returned from the Margin, he had maintained a distance from his friend and co-worker. Not that her presence was unwelcome — more that he needed time to reorder his world.

"Hurry!" Makineng said. "You're going to be late for the announcement, you silly man! Don't you want to be there when the Academy's Grand Kuchiners call your name?"

Pempasigle finished smoothing the cloth over the wooden figurine in his hand and set both on the counter. "Just making my prayers to the patrons. You wouldn't want me to offend them, now, would you?"

Makineng pushed her way into his line of sight. "You've had two weeks to say your prayers. Honestly, I think you do these things just to infuriate me."

"I do enjoy seeing how red your face can get," he said, with a teasing smile.

"Wicked!" she said. "Fine, if you do not have the sense to —"

When he took her hands, all the feistiness dissolved. Her gaze went from his face to his hands, touching her own with such care, such intimacy.

"Makineng, no matter what happens today, I want you to know that you are very dear to me." His heart beat faster. It was his mother's voice in his head now, guiding him on. "Perhaps I will win and go on to be a Grand Kuchiner. Or perhaps I will not, and I will have to keep working my way up as I always have. It doesn't matter to me. Cooking is my gift and my joy and always will be. But my love … my love is you. You are home to me."

Makineng's bright eyes sparkled, her grin stretched, and then she laughed.

"My declaration of love is funny?" he said.

"*You* are funny. I thought you would never find the courage to admit your affection."

"You knew?"

Makineng's tilted head said, *Of course I knew.*

"All this time, I've been waiting for you to stop treating me like some unattainable work of art," she said.

He could only gape.

"You are the strangest man, Pempasigle. You run off to the Margin for your magic plants, come back bruised and broke and empty-handed, but suddenly you're filled with confidence." She leaned in and planted a firm kiss on his cheek. "There. I love you too. Better?"

He released her hands, his body went slack. Then, he grabbed her shoulders and pulled her in close for a real kiss. The sensation reminded him of his first taste of the Vessel of Tears but in a different, more solid way. This was not memories; this was the future. This was hope.

"Better," he said.

Foreheads pressed together, they laughed in time.

"Maki, I will tell you the story of my trip to the Margin. I want there to be no secrets between us."

"Oh, you have secrets?" Makineng asked.

"We all do," he said. "But I believe it is time for truth."

"I think I like this new Pempasigle." She kissed his nose. "Shall we go hear the announcement?"

"Yes."

Pempasigle released her hand, retrieved the wooden figurine, and placed it on the shelf next to the thirteen others. It stood out, with the two swooping horns. He was no carver, but he thought he had captured the likeness well enough.

"What is that?" Makineng asked.

"The fourteenth patron," he said.

"Fourteen?"

"Fourteen, yes. That is Dor, patron of truth."

Kristene Perron

Pulp Literature: *You're a woman of many talents, Kristene. How does such a busy woman find time to write?*

Kristene Perron: Time Turner? Or the real answer, which is that I've always been busy and often on the move so I've developed strategies to keep my writing a priority. My number one strategy is saying, "No." I limit the number of activities I do and groups I get involved in, no matter how tempting. It's easy to lose writing time by degrees — this event is only for one day, going out for coffee with a friend will only take an hour, etc. I have to be a bit of Grinch at times but it works. My husband is also incredibly supportive and has adjusted to being 'ignored' on a regular basis.

PL: *How did you find* Pulp Literature *and make first contact with our magazine?*

KP: I first heard of *Pulp Literature* through SF Canada (Speculative Fiction Canada), which I joined in 2013. At the time, I was consumed by the series I co-author and wasn't working on short fiction but over the years I've read the magazine and gotten to know some of the folks behind the scenes. At the Creative Ink Festival, in Burnaby, BC, I've been thrilled to moderate and sit on a panel about women warriors with JM Landels for the past three years. I was impressed with *Pulp Literature*'s stories, the art, and the people who make it all happen. I always knew I wanted to be a part of this community and, luckily, I just happened to have a story ready when the submission window opened.

PL: *Your main character is a convincing chef. Do you also love to cook?*

KP: Somewhere, beyond the grave, my mother is laughing. I once called her from my university dorm to ask how to make a can of soup. When I turned forty, I decided it was high time I learned to cook more than canned food. It turns out I'm a decent cook and I love trying new recipes. I've also started gardening for the first time this year and get a kick out of cooking the food I grow. I guess I'm a late bloomer.

PL: *Which character do you identify with most in your story?*

KP: Can I say all of them but at different times? Okay, probably Pempasigle most of all. I spent my youth in a safe suburban bubble and when I finally broke out and started travelling, my naive idealism received a swift backhand from reality. I'm still an optimist, and too enthusiastic for my own good, but stepping off the beaten path changes you in ways you can't predict. Much like Pempasigle, experiencing the less-than-pleasant truths of life made me a better person.

PL: *Your novel* Warpworld *is co-written with Joshua Simpson. Does this story take place in the same world?*

KP: Warpworld is set in multiple worlds, since the premise is interdimensional piracy, but not in Pempasigle's world. (Though, theoretically, his world *could* be part of the Warpworld universe). The first Warpworld novel takes place in the worlds of our two heroes,

Seg and Ama. Seg's people are high-tech pirates, robbing other worlds (and worse) to save their own dying planet. Ama is one of the 'primitives' Seg encounters on his first mission across the dimensions. Sparks fly when our heroes meet — figuratively and literally — and an epic adventure begins! The fifth and final book in the series, *Forbidden Revelations*, will be out this year.

PL: *How do you find the co-writing process? Is it easier than going solo?*

KP: I've loved writing with Josh, even if it meant I had to learn to speak Texan. Co-authoring is easier than writing solo in some ways and more difficult in others. On the plus side, being accountable to another writer means there's little room for procrastination. If my partner expects me to be in front of my computer at 9 am, I better be there and ready to work. And we have fun tossing plot curveballs at each other.

On the minus side, scheduling two busy people is tricky. There's also the annoying fact that Josh refuses to concede that I am always right.

PL: *What is your most memorable meal?*

KP: Chandler's restaurant, Seattle, November 1997. Chocolate pâté with a raspberry coulis. Ecstasy.

Selected Bibliography

Novels
Warpworld, Warpworld Vol. 1 (2012)
Wasteland Renegades, Warpworld Vol. 2 (2013)
Ghost World, Warpworld Vol. 3 (2015)
Final Storm, Warpworld Vol. 4 (2016)
Forbidden Revelations, Warpworld Vol. 5 (2018)

Short Fiction
'Lucky Me' (*Denizens of Darkness,* 2012)
'Unity Tested', Warpworld Shadow Story (2013) Novelette
'Birds Also Cry' (2014)
'Place of Others', Warpworld Shadow Story (2016) Novelette
'Safe Harbour' (*Escape Pod,* 2017)

THE MAGPIE AWARD FOR POETRY

THE MAGPIE AWARD FOR POETRY

We're always excited to see what shiny poems our Magpie Poetry Contest brings back to the nest. Of our shortlist, three poems caught Renée Sarojini Saklikar's eye for the fifth annual Magpie Award for Poetry. Like the bird this contest is named after, these poems are smart, bold, and flashy.

2nd Runner-up
'My desk' by Angela Caravan
"An ambitious poem, which needs some attention to line breaks and form. That being said, the language intrigues. The possibility of what the language is attempting here: admirable." — *Renée Saklikar*

First Runner-up
'ALL I NEED IS A CHAIR, MY RED PIANO, AND'
by Christine Leviczky Riek
"I enjoyed the dense construction, which leads reader into the world of the poem, telling a story of loss and longing, using repetition of key phrases and a great evocation of a particular time and place." — *RS*

Winner
'Leather wraps both our shoulders, and I will call you my lungs, my falconer, guidepost' by Kelli Allen
"I read this lovely poem as a sonnet with its fourteen-line construction and those interesting, rhythmic two-line couplets cascading a series of stories in image. Wonderful!" — *R*

The 2018 Magpie Poetry Contest Shortlist

'Leather wraps both our shoulders, and I will call you my lungs, my falconer, guidepost' *by Kelli Allen*
'My desk' *by Angela Caravan*
'someone comes along with a very bad character' by *Daniela Elza*
'Oral' *by Rula Jurdi*
'College Lesson' *by Charlene Kwiatkowski*
'ALL I NEED IS A CHAIR, MY RED PIANO, AND' *by Christine Leviczky Riek*
'the magpie seasons' *by Scott-Patrick Mitchell*
'Atelier' *by Cara Waterfall*
'The Crocodile Feeder of Yamoussoukro' *by Cara Waterfall*
'Assassination' *by Sarah Zwickle*

Kelli Allen's work has appeared in numerous journals and anthologies in the US and internationally. She has served as Poetry Editor for The Lindenwood Review *and she directs River Styx's Hungry Young Poets Series. She is currently a visiting professor at Northeast Normal University in Changchun, China. Her chapbook,* Some Animals, *won the 2016 Etchings Press Prize. Her chapbook,* How We Disappear, *won the 2016 Damfino Press award. Her full-length poetry collection,* Otherwise, Soft White Ash, *arrived from John Gosslee Books (2012) and was nominated for the Pulitzer Prize. Her latest collection,* Imagine Not Drowning, *was released by C&R Press in January 2017.* www.kelli-allen.com

LEATHER WRAPS BOTH OUR SHOULDERS, AND I WILL CALL YOU MY LUNGS, MY FALCONER, GUIDEPOST

BY KELLI ALLEN

We have swallowed the whole field. Tell me how to discover shovels leaning less still, their names for metals happening later, closer to dusk.

I would give you buildings on fire, barn house doors ashed to moss, if you threw one hand into the pond, pulled windowpanes back to shore. I know every moment you tighten the other palm around horses kept miniature in my pockets. Our bodies often possessed by place, fit one into the other under stained glass, borrowed warm.

Kingdoms don't need context to nestle further against hillocks. I have been writing our story to measure how underwater, my mouth holds your throat softer, legs

untangling in the last chapter, waking our firebird too late. That past is image over image is no accident. Your jaw aches through each night and October rains anyway.

The doe is a widow. We see her cross one hoof too rough into woodpecker nests fallen before anything autumnal pronounced an hour for grief, or for sleeping.

Eventually, we accept stars' light as distance side-by-side. Abundance is forgiving, is the carpet under my knees, and your chin dawn-lit, eyes closed against everything.

Christine Leviczky Riek *is a poet and photographer from Surrey, BC. In search of an uncle she never met, this poem became her discovery of crossed paths, unknown connections, parallel lives, missed chances. The poem's form is her interpretation of an Alexandrine sonnet, inspired by Lajos Galánffy, a poet ancestor who worked in Hungarian.*

ALL I NEED IS A CHAIR, MY RED PIANO, AND

BY CHRISTINE LEVICZKY RIEK

out there above the window red berries on the
spotted laurel dappling shade on the yard walkway's
scored space, blank space with four minor flats in Chopin's
ballade number four and soon I'm walking from that
old hotel to buy some grapes on saint dominique
eighty metres mostly flat, in their brown paper
bag stamped red and green, my uncle to cimetière
five hundred and fifty steps, yet we never met
there at père lachaise; my chair is on an april
train with my eurail youthpass, my old body sat

in this new world, my heart lost in that old one, and
on the road to fontainebleau I find my uncle
buried in a pauper's grave, the train leaves every
thirty minutes though Chopin plays a lifetime in
twelve and all I can manage is to pay twelve francs
for a thirty-minute bath at gare de lyon
stroll three kilometres on the sidewalk past the
passage de folie, the rue du repos to reach
the chemin vert, where my uncle once lived, along
the dappled green path outside my basement window

Angela Caravan writes poetry and fiction. She lives in Vancouver, BC, with a boy and a man and sometimes has trouble telling the difference between the two. You can find some of her recent writing in Longleaf Review and Reel Honey Mag. Twitter: @a_caravan

My desk

BY ANGELA CARAVAN

Furniture that exudes femininity
The soft curve of brushed metal
And the current fad of white
On wood. Then sits there, beautifully, with
a pile of papers
     in one corner.

  That is your lost potential

Command it to kick up legs and wander
Or commence perpetual wading, though the prospect
Turns stomachs.

A pitcher plant
Memento from your predecessor that says
to keep going through the rough and
Laugh heartily at the lesson.

This is your lost fortitude

Not classified a syndrome. This that
Disallows you from being wrong,
Existing and working through ache then
Drink teas to cast spells of comfort.

A computer mouse
Fit for all hands and the cushion you found to
Protect yourself. In it, your bodily moans.
The aches in joints that grow to exhaustion
By day's end, it is filled with powdered marrow.

Framed photos
To remind you of your failings as a parent

Here is your absent intention

The division of your time across spreadsheets
In moments you've lost, read incantations to preserve

Time spent at desk.
   Worthless, toppled post,
   with a porcelain cat.

AWAY GAME

Mitchell Toews

Mitchell Toews *lives and writes at Jessica Lake in Manitoba. When an insufficient number of, "We are pleased to inform you . . ." emails are on hand he finds alternative joy in the windy intermingling between the top of the water and the bottom of the sky or skates on the ice until he can no longer see the cabin. Mitch's writing has appeared in* riverbabble, CommuterLit, Fiction on the Web, Literally Stories, Red Fez, SickLit, Voices Journal, The Machinery, Storgy, LingoBites, Work magazine, Occulum, Rhubarb Magazine, *and* Fictive Dream *(November 2017).*

$\mathcal{A}$WAY GAME

My great-great-grandfather came to visit us at the lake. This was unexpected because he had died ninety years earlier.

He spoke in a Mennonite *haferlschuh* with short demanding sentences and syntax reminiscent of a buggy ride over frozen stubble. Clear eyes stared you down into the blackened remnants of a failed Red Fife wheat crop.

"That's some beard you have there," I said.

"Call me Opa," he said. "Why don't you have a beard?"

"Too itchy," I replied.

He stared at the lake. "Why are you living here? What's wrong with town?"

"We like it here, Opa. How is it where you are?" I asked, half-rising to adjust my lawn chair.

"It gets terrible hot and smells like sewer gas, but the women sure are sporty," he said. Then he took a long sip of his drink, eyes merry over the rim of the glass while he regarded me. Janice, standing behind my chair, misted me with lemonade as she burst out laughing.

"He told me to say that if you asked. That is such a funny guy," he said.

Opa was a former church deacon. He was the delegate selected to come to Canada to choose the land on which the Molotschna Mennonites would settle. Bearded and bonneted, my ancestors left in a staggered diaspora when the friendly steppes of Catherine the Great became unwelcoming. Following his journey in 1874, the migration continued until 1920, more or less.

Death agreed with Opa. He looked exactly like he did in the crinkled black-and-white pictures from the shoebox in our closet. He showed off a fine set of store-bought choppers.

I kept playing it straight. "You are with the Lord?" I said.

"Well, it's not exactly like that, but I'm not supposed to tell. They don't let us."

"*Nah jo,*" I replied, slipping into *Plattdeutsch*—Low German—for his benefit while wondering who exactly *they* were.

There's no language where I am," he said in his matter-of-fact way. "No religion either."

As I considered this, he hawked his throat extra loud and regrouped. "Derwin says *gn'dach*. He says you guys were buddies." It came out sounding like 'bodies' because of his big accent; the vowels flattened like fresh horse shit under a cartwheel.

I thought back to my friend Derwin. I remembered him sitting in the pub with us after basketball one evening. He had come out to join us—his first and last time—and sat in his new, tight-fitting tracksuit drinking rye and Coke. He told me stories about our shared relative, "Delegate Zehen." Larger than life, or death, this slender man (*kjrenkjlich denn ooda schwak*—skinny; looking under-fed) was my great-great-opa and Derwin's great-great-uncle. My friend Derwin had been an historian before his untimely passing.

Opa hummed and smacked his lips, looking again at the far shore. He seemed restless. "Got any smokes? Dere's no smoking up dere," he said, jabbing a crooked thumb skyward. "I miss tobacco, a bit."

Janice began walking towards the cabin. "I'll get you one," she said over her shoulder.

We were quiet until she got back. Opa stared at me the whole time. I could hear him talking to himself, but his lips weren't moving. "This woman of his smokes. That shouldn't surprise me, but still—it's terrible *weltlich*. I remember some of those stuck-up Winnipeg *freundshaft* women smoked. Oh-but. *Winnipegsch!*"

Not disturbed by the telepathy, I struggled to translate. My Plattdeutsch was like a favourite hat plucked from my head by the Salish Sea wind, floating away in the breeze beyond the fantail of the Tsawwassen ferry. *Weltlich* was 'worldly', *freundshaft* was 'family' or 'relatives'. *Winnipegsch* stumped me. I was about to ask him when he said aloud, "*Winnipegsch?* That's fancy things or how some people act in Winnipeg—like they are too big for their *bekj*."

"Thanks," I said. *Bekj*, or *bekjen*, was 'pants', or maybe 'britches'.

"I missed you. Did you know that?" Opa said, pale blue eyes drilling at me.

"But Opa, we never met. I mean, you died before I was born."

"Yeah, I know. That made it worse!" he said, rocking forward in his chair.

He did seem lonely. But it was hard to judge. I felt headachy, and my chest hurt.

"It's not really lonely," said the voice in my head—Opa's voice. "More like a longing. Desire for the familiar; craving for people and things you loved well."

I thought of my middle-school friend, waiting on a pile of discarded tires beside the abandoned shed where we took turns feeling Tina's breasts, her blouse unbuttoned, lips moist. I looked at my hand, now inexplicably holding my favourite finishing hammer, the one with the wood handle and the sharply cleft bell and the delicate, patinaed steel. I grasped what Opa's voice was telling me, manifested in a flood of long-forgotten thoughts.

"*Nah ja,*" he said as he accepted a light from Janice and inhaled until the tip of the cigarette crackled. "Do you have skates?" he said to me, nodding a thank you to Janice.

Puzzled, I glanced at the dragonflies darting above us. When I looked back at Opa, he was surrounded by a team of hockey players. They had emerged from the cattails. Derwin, my dad, WP Kinsella, Redd Foxx, and my father-in-law were there with my uncle Ken.

"We got a game at two," Opa said, pulling on a ragged hockey glove. The palm — thin as doe skin — was cut out with painstaking care, so he could grip the stick with his bare hand. I could feel the air taking on a coolness. It smelled like our old hockey rink: wet leather and exhaust fumes from the Massey tractor that flooded the ice.

"He's our goalie, so you can play out," Opa said.

He handed me an old CCM stick and a roll of black tape.

Okay, I thought. I guess I'll play out.

GROSS MOTOR

Sara Mang

*Originally from Labrador, **Sara** was an artillery officer in the Canadian Forces before retiring to be at home with her three children. In 2017, Sara's short stories were finalists for numerous awards including* The New Quarterly's Peter Hinchcliffe Award *and the* Disquiet International Literary Prize. *She is currently an MFA candidate in UBC's Creative Writing Program.*

Gross Motor

Patty's migraine started as she read the morning paper with sunlight shooting through her window. *Archeologists unearth massive statue in Cairo slum.* In her kindergarten classroom, her students sit cross-legged on the floor, looking up at her like she's a rainbow. Red, blue and green circles, triangles and squares; primary colours are everywhere and acrylic paint smells like new carpet. A stream of yellow-green mucus folds out of Carson's nose and he smudges it away with his sleeve. Monday is *lundi* in French, but these children don't speak French, nor do they understand it. Patty must immerse them in secondary language and primary colours.

Massive bedbug infestation uncovered at Aurora Apartments. Little Abby's hair is a matted nest which she scratches violently. Last week, she was sent home with head lice. The tiny bugs crawled on her scalp and on the shaft of her blonde hair, laying eggs, sucking blood. Patty points to the calendar. "Quelle saison?" Faces upturn, mouths open, like worm-hungry birds. Patty breathes deeply through her nose. They don't understand. Sometimes she mutters profanities just to keep herself entertained. She calls them fleas or cabbages, which are endearing terms in French, but she secretly deletes the endearing part. 'Ma puce' or 'mon petit chou'. The season is autumn. The school year is fat. An ache creeps behind her ears, lays eggs, sucks blood. Her scalp warms beneath the fluorescent lights. She closes her eyes for just a moment. "Juste un moment. S'il vous plait."

Hurricane Enew continues to produce a large area of swelling seas as it moves slowly over the North Atlantic.

"Madame, Alex is on my square," Carson whimpers, his voice nasal and musical.

"Madame, Carson said poop." Alex pushes Carson, who bumps Abby, whose elbow clips Jacob in the eye. Jacob wails.

Train runs twenty kilometres without driver. Probe ordered.

"Yoga. Yes. Calm. En français — *calme*. Tout le monde?" The children stand, arms swing, fingers poke.

"Touchez pas. Soyez *calme*."

"Arbre." Patty's breathing races as she positions herself in tree pose. She is a swaying tree. The students attempt to fix feet to thighs. They lean. Some fall. Patty's stomach hurls.

Causeway collapses in Oklahoma. Hundreds buried beneath the rubble.

"Knock, knock." Principal Tyson is conducting a parent tour. "... French immersion kindergarten program ... best in the city ... natural light in this classroom ... blinding."

Patty raises her hands above her head and tells her students to breathe through their noses and lean to the left. "À gauche tout le monde." They lean and peek at their visitors.

"Here we assess gross motor skills through yoga." Principal Tyson manoeuvres the parents to the next class as they nod and nudge in approval. "Yoga also fosters a formidable connection between teacher and student."

Russian airstrike in Syria hits US Allies by mistake.

Patty exhales. The room is vignetted then dark. Echoes.

"Madame?" Abby scratches as she looks at her teacher on the floor.

Carson shrugs and wipes his nose with his sleeve. "She's napping, I think."

SMALL TOWN SUPERHERO

Dave Beynon

Dave Beynon's stories have appeared in periodicals and anthologies, received an honourable mention in The Best Horror of the Year, and he was shortlisted for the inaugural Terry Pratchett Prize. He grew up on farmland in Southern Ontario and now lives in a small town outside of Toronto with his family. Sadly, his small town doesn't have a superhero. His website is davebeynon.com.

Small Town Superhero

Last week, Captain Invincible came to town.

It wasn't a social call.

As mayor, officially greeting Canada's greatest superhero fell directly into the *other duties as they arise* column of my elected role. An hour before his unannounced arrival, an entourage comprised of his agent, his assistant, and some sort of government representative stormed our municipal offices.

I was out at Polston's Dairy Farm helping Ivan try to turn a breech calf. I was considering the choice betweens chains or a caesarean when my phone rang. Ivan's daughter Marta took the call since I was shoulder-deep in Holstein at the time.

"Tell them I'll be there as soon as I can," I said, coaxing a back leg in the right direction.

Marta rolled her eyes, and nobody rolls their eyes like a teenager. "Captain Invincible's agent says it's important. Says you need to be there when he arrives." I looked over the back of the cow and motioned, with my own roll of the eyes and a tip of my head, that Marta should bring the phone closer. She held it next to my ear.

"Who's this, then?" I asked. There was a sucking sound as the calf shifted a bit more.

"I'm Andrew Carter. I represent Captain Invincible. You really must get here for when he arrives."

"Must I, now? Really? Listen, Mr Carter. I don't recall an appointment booked for today, with or without a superhero. Quick question: Let's say I came down to Toronto. If I wanted to see Mr Invincible, how far in advance would I have to make an appointment?"

"It's *Captain* Invincible, and one does not simply make an appointment."

"Sorry. *Captain*—wouldn't want to damage the brand. Anyway, I'm no Captain Invincible, but I am the mayor of this little town. I'm always happy to meet with folks, but you need to understand: mayor of a municipality the size of Mitchell's Crossing isn't exactly a full-time job. I'm also a vet and right now, as I speak to you, in fact, I have both arms inside a prize-winning dairy cow—one right up to the shoulder—trying to save her and her calf. You'll forgive me, but these cattle and Mr Polson's livelihood are just a smidge more important than some superhero's damaged ego and his unannounced visit. If you're nice and ask politely, I'm sure our town clerk can direct you to one of the three excellent cafés just a short walk away from the township offices. You can enjoy a coffee and a nice slice of pie while you wait."

"The Captain will be arriving within the hour."

"Can't check my watch right now, Mr Carter. If I'm done, I'm done, and I'll be there in time. If I'm not, well … tell me. Captain Invincible's bulletproof, right?"

"Y-yes …"

"Then waiting a few minutes until I get there isn't likely to kill him, is it?" With a nod of my head, I told Marta to hang up on him. A few moments later, with the right combination of coaxing, leverage, and gravity, a fine heifer calf spilled with a wet thump onto the floor by my feet. Always a rare treat when you can get the job done without resorting to the chains or a scalpel.

After a wash and a quick cup of coffee with the Polsons, I climbed into my truck with plenty of time to make it to the parking lot behind the municipal building in time to witness the arrival of the mighty Captain Invincible. Already annoyed at the nature of my summoning to the township office, I cringed and counted to ten when the tire inflation light on my dashboard lit up. Tony, the best mechanic a little town could ask for, had reset the damn thing just two days before. I made a mental note to slip over to his garage a little later to have him look at it … again.

I walked around to the lawn of Mitchell Square to see half the town assembled, all looking upwards. I sidled up to Brenda, our town clerk, and whispered in her ear.

"So," I asked, "where's the asshole I was speaking to on the phone?"

"That would be the asshole with the iPad standing next to Eddie and Carol."

Eddie and Carol are reporters-slash-photographers for our two competing newspapers. One is a town paper, *The Record,* and the other is a countywide newspaper, *The Herald.* It figured that a superhero's agent would waste no time getting the local press in on the action.

"Thanks, Brenda. Off to work, I suppose."

"Eddie," I said with a nod. "Carol." I extended my hand to Captain Invincible's agent. "And you must be Mr Carter. I'm Mike Brewer. We spoke on the phone."

Carter dubiously eyed my hand.

"Oh, for God's sake," I said. "I wear gloves that come up to my ear. Besides, I've washed it since we last spoke."

Reluctantly, he took my hand. His shake was as limp as a noodle.

"Really, Mayor Brewer, you cut things a little close."

"I didn't cut anything any which way at all. I told you I was doing a job and that I'd be here when I'd be here. I'm here, and now I'm at liberty to check my watch. Look at that. Your client is late."

Carter bristled. "Captain Invincible is never late."

As if on cue, a roar went up from the crowd. Streaking from the south just above the rooftops was a blur of red and white. The blur slowed and circled our municipal building. Captain Invincible, in his uniform of skin-tight armour and fluttering cape, hovered over the crowd, waving as he slowly descended. I felt the stir of electricity shimmering in the air around him as he touched down an arm's length from me.

"Good afternoon, people of Marshall's Crossing," boomed the voice we all recognized from dozens of government-sponsored public service announcements. Just hearing the timbre of his words made me want to spay or neuter any number of household pets.

"Mitchell's," I said.

"I beg your pardon?" The tone of Captain Invincible's question led me to believe he wasn't often corrected.

"*Mitchell's* Crossing. You've just touched down in *Mitchell's* Crossing, not Marshall's Crossing. Common enough mistake, I suppose, though I've never heard anyone make it before." I extended my hand. "I'm Mike Brewer. I'm the mayor of this little town."

Though most of his face was hidden by his mask, the smile I could see was forced. He shook my hand. Unlike his agent, there was strength in that grip. If the stories were true, that hand could have crushed mine into sausage meat. I sensed a part of him would have enjoyed doing just that. Instead, he turned that forced smile into a practised grin and hammed it up for the crowd.

"I am pleased to meet you, Mayor Brewer. Good people of Mitchell's Crossing, I have urgent business with your mayor. I have asked my people to set up an autograph signing for later. Mr Mayor, is there a place we may speak in private?"

"Just call me Mike. There's my office, but I've got to tell you, I have no idea what any of this is about."

Casting a glance at his agent and assistant, the Captain placed a hand on my shoulder and leaned in to whisper.

"You've not been briefed?"

"I just got here myself. Didn't fly here, though. I came in my truck. Is this something to do with crime? If it is, I think I ought to call Lydia in to the meeting with us."

"Lydia?"

"Lydia Niven. She's the staff sergeant with our local OPP detachment. She's just over there."

"Perhaps that would be best," he said. "Local law enforcement always likes to feel like they are doing something."

Waving to Lydia, I beckoned her to follow us into the municipal building. When I looked behind me and realized the Captain had brought all three members of his entourage, I decided to move the meeting into council chambers. Taking my usual seat, I motioned the others to sit where they liked.

"So," I said when everyone seemed comfortable, "what's Canada's mightiest superhero doing in Mitchell's Crossing?"

Captain Invincible raised a gloved finger and appeared about to speak when he was silenced by a gentle 'ahem' from the government representative sitting to his left. She leaned forward, looking at me over the top of her wireframe glasses.

"We haven't been introduced. I'm Lian Bai, Captain Invincible's governmental liaison officer. Tell me, Mayor Brewer, what do you know about the Enhanced Power Being Regulation Act of 1992?"

"Please," I said, "it's Mike. Nice to meet you. I don't know a lot about the EPB Act except that it seems to want to compartmentalize EPB people. Never been a big fan of compartmentalizing people, super-powered or otherwise. You?"

She shrugged. "It's kind of my job. The act states that any and all EPBs who exhibit substantial or potentially dangerous EP abilities must be assessed by a governmental representative—that would be me—in the presence of a certified and trusted EPB of the same or higher EP ability level—that would be the Captain."

"That's a mouthful. Can you define *substantial* and *potentially dangerous* for me?"

She smiled. "It's like pornography—I'll know it when I see it."

"No offence, but that's hardly a definition to base legislation on—I speak as a legislator myself in this instance. That aside, let's go back to my original question: Why are you folks in Mitchell's Crossing?"

Captain Invincible raised his finger once more, and this time Ms Bai let him speak.

"Mayor Brewer … Mike, two weeks ago there was a fire just outside of your town."

"At our car parts factory, yes. Half the plant went up in flames before our volunteer fire department was able to get it under control. Trident Metal Fab is our township's single biggest employer. A lot of folks are feeling the pinch until the plant is up and running again. That fire hurt our local economy plenty. Fortunately, no one was seriously hurt in the blaze."

"We received information that there were people trapped in the plant."

I shifted in my chair. "That's true … kind of. There were six people trapped for a while in the machine shop at one side of the plant. They were able to escape with only minor burns and a little smoke inhalation. It would have been great to have a superhero like you here two weeks ago to help us put that fire out. Or at least help with the clean-up afterwards. Hell of a mess."

"We have reason to believe that there was an EPB at that fire who rescued those trapped workers."

I glanced over at Lydia.

"Really? You were there the night of the fire. Did you see any superheroes, Lydia?"

She shook her head. "Nope. You were there, too, Mike. Did you see any that I might have missed?"

"Not a one. Just a whole bunch of volunteer firefighters and public works employees who did their best work that night so that there's still a plant that can be repaired and keep folks employed. So, Captain, how about you tell me why you believe we had a superhero at that fire."

"There was a video," said Ms Bai, "posted to Facebook."

I sat in stunned silence. I let it drag on just long enough that the superhero and his entourage started to fidget.

"Facebook?" I asked. "You and these three people have come all the way out here from New York over a video posted on Facebook? Facebook?"

Extending her hand, Ms Bai turned in her chair towards the agent. "Andrew." He handed her his iPad. She made a few swipes, then handed me the tablet. Lydia leaned closer to watch.

On the screen was a shaky scene, obviously shot on someone's phone. It was a good distance beyond the police cars, fire engines, and a pair of Mitchell's Crossing Public Works trucks. There were a number of people I recognized gathered around. In the distance was Trident Metal Fab, a full third of the building engulfed in flames. I watched as a section of the wall beneath the burning roof exploded outwards, cinderblocks cartwheeling onto the asphalt of the parking lot. Through the hole, a person wearing coveralls and a snowmobile helmet carried a pair of coughing, injured workers. The person in the coveralls deposited the pair a safe distance from the fire, then vanished in a smearing blur of speed back into the building. Over the next ten seconds, all six workers were pulled from the blaze. Once the last two were deposited next to their fellows, the person in the coveralls regarded the crowd, looked upwards, then shot straight up out of the frame, a ripple of distortion fanning outwards from where he'd stood.

"Wow," I said. "That's pretty well done. Especially the part where the guy in the helmet flies straight up at the end."

"Only one problem, though," said Lydia. "None of that happened."

"What do you mean?" asked Ms Bai. "It's all right there. We've analyzed the video. That is Trident Metal, and the date on the video is the date of your factory's fire."

"Analyze and authenticate all you want," I said. "Lydia and I were there. I was there when those six people came out of the fire. Through a rolling garage door. They were walking together, leaning on one another for support, except for the Jones kid. What's his name?"

"Trevor," said Lydia. "He was the one who was struck by some falling debris. Helped out by Jim Taylor and Alice Vandermole."

"Trevor Jones. That's right. The door they came through is just outside the frame of this video. Probably about twenty feet to the right. I don't know what to say."

"It looks like you've fallen victim to a hoax," said Lydia. "If you give me the details of the video — whose account it came from, how it came to your attention, your video analysis — I can open a docket towards a possible nuisance complaint. If that's how you want to proceed."

Captain Invincible stood. "That is not how we want to proceed. This video clearly illustrates that there is a potentially powerful and dangerous EPB in your community. I would think that you, as mayor, would show some concern."

"And what exactly would this EPB's superpower be? Doctoring video recordings? I told you that both the staff sergeant and I were at that fire. We both agree that the events on that video never happened."

"There are many people in the foreground of that recording. I assume they are residents of this town. I assume you recognize some of them."

I nodded. "I'm not doubting that there was video footage shot during the fire. I think half the bystanders had their phones out. I know that both Carol and Eddie — those are the reporters for our local papers that your agent was talking with earlier — were there snapping pictures and talking to the crowd. And yes, I can put a name to at least half the people appearing in that video you just showed us. Probably more than half. I'm not doubting that video was shot the night of the fire. I'm just saying that it's been altered to show some superheroics that never happened."

Captain Invincible glanced at Ms Bai. She stood and took a step towards me.

"You do realize, Mayor Brewer," she said, casting what I'm sure she thought was a threatening look in my direction, "that according to the EPB Regulation Act, harbouring or giving safe haven to an unregistered EPB of substantial ability is a criminal offence."

I sighed and leaned back in my chair.

"I realize no such thing," I said. "And there you go with your undefined *substantial* again. I'm not harbouring anyone. *Harbouring*—what does that mean anyway? The long and short of it is that the video has been altered. You're showing us special effects."

"Our people have analyzed the video and found no evidence of tampering."

"And I was there and tell you none of that happened. This is just silly. You're here to do what, exactly? Locate and identify a person in a YouTube video posted on Facebook? A faked video, at that."

"It's authentic," Ms Bai said. "I assure you."

"Assure me all you want. You could have your tech person swear on a stack of Bibles—a stack so high that Captain Invincible here would have to fly him up there to put his hand on the top—and say the video hasn't been altered, and though I know nothing at all about video editing, I'd tell that technician to his face that he's wrong."

"We believe you are harbouring the person in that video."

"To what end, Ms Bai?"

"That's what we need to know."

"We're getting nowhere. Lydia, what's the legal status of this little meeting we're having, from your point of view as a police officer?"

Lydia smiled. I'd known it would be a good idea to have her tag along.

"Not many people realize this, but superheroes like Captain Invincible here have very limited powers under the law. He has only those powers of a regular citizen when it comes to detention and making a citizen's arrest, although in practice, superheroes are often given some leniency given their particular abilities. Since he is accompanying a government representative on official business, it might be argued that he has the same authority as myself or any police officer during the course of his or her duties. This interview, if that's what this is, is entirely voluntary, and you or I may request it be terminated at any time. If this is an official investigation, however, Captain Invincible would have been well-served to advise us of our right to have legal counsel present during this interview."

"Is that so?" I turned towards the Captain and Ms Bai. "But this was never meant to be anything so grand as an official investigation, was it? You just had a couple of questions about a video. I have to admit, that video does look real. I can understand why you'd be concerned. If I hadn't been at the fire myself, I would be the first person trying to get to the bottom of things.

"Listen, I don't know where you hail from, Captain, or you, Ms Bai, or you, Mr Carter, or you, young lady at the end of the table no one bothered to introduce to me, but I've lived here all my life. If there was a superhero in our midst, I'd know it. That video is faked, and to put your minds at rest, I have a suggestion.

"Take the afternoon to visit our little community. Walk around. Get a snack. Spend some money at our local shops. People love it when out-of-towners stimulate our local economy. Especially after the fire, our storeowners could use all the custom they can get. People around here will get a big kick out of having their pictures taken with Captain Invincible. While you're at it, chat with the people—folks on the street, the shopkeepers, everyone and anyone. Ask around. Show people the video and hear what they have to say. Those who were at the fire will tell you what I told you. As exciting as it might be, places like Mitchell's Crossing just don't have superheroes."

"Aren't you even curious about who posted the video?" asked Captain Invincible.

I shrugged. "Not particularly, but I'm pretty sure I can guess. It will either be Danny Robinson or Amy Tarkington." I noticed Ms Bai's eyebrow rise when I mentioned the Tarkington girl's name. "You know how I know that? Every year there's this school competition called Digifest. It's a moviemaking competition that runs from grade six or seven right up to grade twelve. Kids try their hands at putting together a short film that's judged first at the school, then regionally, then at the provincial level. Last year I had my picture in the paper with Danny and Amy holding the plaque they received when they took Digifest gold in the Ontario Elementary School Division. Ha. Sorry, guys. You've been had by a couple of very talented small-town teenage moviemakers."

Captain Invincible and his entourage took my advice. Walking around town, Captain Invincible shook hands and signed autographs on the streets. They got ice cream cones and some fudge from our chocolate shop. The Captain held an impromptu book signing at Roxy's Books and Gifts, clearing out Roxy's entire stock of *Maple Leaf Hero: The Captain Invincible Story*. For every autograph signed, another local was questioned about the fire and the video. When they finished touring downtown, Lydia took the entourage to speak with both Danny and Amy who, after apologizing for the confusion, confirmed that this year's Digifest entry was apt to take gold in the prestigious High School Junior Division.

It was late afternoon before I shook hands with Captain Invincible in Mitchell Square so that Eddie and Carol would have a decent picture for this week's paper. Taking my business card, the Captain promised to call if he had any other questions, then, nodding to the gathered crowd, flew off towards the south and east, home to Toronto. His entourage climbed into their SUV without saying goodbye. As I watched their tail lights disappear, I decided I'd had enough of folks from the city for one day.

On the way back to my vet clinic, I decided to stop in at Tony's Automotive and have that low inflation light checked. Tony greeted me as I climbed from the truck, wiping his oily hands on the legs of his coveralls.

"Hey, Mr Big Shot Mayor," he said, offering me his hand, then, seeing it was still dirty, pulled it back. "What brings you out to my corner of town?"

I walked with him into the garage and poured myself a mug of coffee from his pot. I dropped a dollar into the tin that helped pay to keep the grounds fresh.

"You don't have to pay," Tony said, filling a mug for himself.

"No special favours just because I'm mayor."

"Jesus, you only started paying for your coffee *after* you became mayor, Mike. Besides, that tin can is hardly more than wishful thinking. Nobody pays for coffee except for you and Mrs Rutledge."

"That flat tire wheel light thing came on again. I thought you'd fixed that."

Tony rubbed his chin. "I thought I had, too. I'll check your tire pressure, but I think the sensor's probably screwed. The smarter they try to make these cars, the dumber they get." Tony pulled a tire gauge from his coveralls' breast pocket and started for the door. He motioned for me to follow.

"Hey," he said as he knelt by my front left tire, "I heard there was some excitement around town today. What was that all about?"

"You heard?"

"Of course I heard. It's a small town. What's he like?"

"Captain Invincible? Shorter than you'd imagine. I don't know what that outfit of his is made of, but it's awfully shiny. He was okay, I guess. There was this officious government person—some superhero liaison thing. She seemed a little stiff but was nice enough. I think she got a little irked when she couldn't intimidate me, though. His agent seemed to be a bit of an asshole."

"Oh, yeah?" Tony had moved on to the next tire. "How so?"

"I was out at Polson's place helping with a breech, and the agent calls up demanding my presence."

"Demanding? Nice. Say—you going to be heading back out there? By the Polson place, I mean."

"I could slip in on my way back to the clinic. I should probably check on that calf. Why?"

Tony tilted his chin towards the little parts counter inside his garage. "Ivan asked me to order in a replacement oil filter for that big new tractor of his, and it arrived this morning. Would you mind dropping it off? It'll just save him a trip in or me a trip out. Only if you're heading that way, though." Tony moved on to the tires on the other side of my truck.

"No problem," I said. "They were here asking about the fire out at Trident."

I couldn't see Tony's face but I detected a subtle change in his voice.

"You don't say," he said. "What for, do you think?"

"They had this crazy notion that we had our very own super-hero here in Mitchell's Crossing. They believed they had evidence that he'd made an appearance at the Trident fire. That he'd rescued those six trapped workers in the machine shop."

Tony stood up on the other side of my truck, tucking the tire gauge back into his breast pocket. "Tires are fine, Mike. I can reset the error light again, but I think there's something wrong with the sensor. I can order a new sensor, but it'll be pricey."

"Don't bother resetting it. Let me know how much a new sensor will cost before you order it in. Look at the time. I guess I will check on Polson's calf before I go to the clinic. You want to get me that oil filter for Ivan?"

Tony grabbed the filter. I traded him my empty coffee mug for it.

"I appreciate you acting as delivery boy for me, Mike," he said. "So you set him straight, right? Captain Invincible, I mean. He won't be coming back?"

Climbing into my truck, I tossed the oil filter on the seat next to me.

"We set him straight, Lydia and me. I doubt we'll get a return visit. Superheroes have no business in places like Mitchell's Crossing, right?"

"You got that right," Tony said, turning and walking back to his garage.

I wound down my window and called out to Tony. He stopped and faced me.

"Oh, one more thing. One little favour, okay, Tony?"

"Anything for you, Mike. What is it?"

"Next time the need arises," I said, "can you please smash through the wall that *isn't* facing the crowd and a dozen witnesses with cameras? It'll just make life a whole lot easier for everyone."

EVERY TOWN HAS ONE

Epiphany Ferrell

Epiphany Ferrell writes most of her fiction in southern Illinois at Resurrection Mule Farm, named for a mule that survived a lightning strike and was, according to sources, never "quite right" afterwards. Her stories appear in a couple dozen venues online and in print, including Ghost Parachute, the Dead Mule School of Southern Literature, Mojave River Review and Cease, Cows. *She is an editor at Flash Fiction Magazine. This story began, as many do, with a drink at a bar — ok, two, maybe three drinks — and the fanciful thoughts that sometimes such combinations inspire. Twitter: @EpiphanyFerrell*

BAR

Every Town Has One

Every town has one: the guy who has been there forever, whom everyone knows by first name, who never seems to change.

Mickey was such a one.

Mickey was a fixture in Oak Heart. He'd always been part of the town, surely, hadn't he? But the town natives, the ones who'd grown up in Oak Heart and never left, didn't remember Mickey as a child. No one could remember having gone to school with him. He wasn't in any of the yearbooks. So he must have shown up one day and so immediately understood the town that he became part of it.

He was present at any outdoor concert, and at any art festival or barbecue. He was almost always drink-in-hand. He seemed to have some sort of police immunity. But then, Mickey never caused anyone any trouble. His distinctive laugh, his "you know what I mean?" refrain, those things might become irritating during the course of a few hours, but never enough to become a police problem.

Everyone knew Mickey's daughter, too. She'd almost always looked the same, same as he did, except for that some people said they could remember when she'd been smaller. But she always had the same long, straight brown hair, and the same long, slender legs, the same brilliant but solemn smile and the knowing eyes.

The boys thronged to Jessie, especially when she'd start dancing. She had a way of twisting her body, her arms in the air twined together, that was reminiscent of belly dancing and of bondage at the same time. She'd close her eyes and bend her body, a soft smile on her lips. Suddenly her eyes would fly open; she'd look at whatever boy was in front of her and break out in delighted laughter, as if they'd just shared a thrilling experience together, like a roller coaster ride. The boy would invariably look dazed, and Jessie would glide like a snake to another corner of the dance floor, her hair flowing over her shoulders like river water.

Sometimes Mickey would get mad. He was a jovial drunk, but sometimes his arm would drop around a boy's shoulders, like pals, and he'd talk in a low voice, the muscles on his forearms and the veins like cords beneath the skin. Then he'd laugh, and it would be all right again, and the boy would steer clear of Jessie for a few weeks. Maybe at the next outdoor concert she'd see him, and she'd playfully stomp a foot or put her hands on her hips and give him a laughing glare and say, "Where have you been?" The boy would look uneasily at Mickey, and Mickey would laugh and tell him which bar they were heading to next and that he should come along there.

Meadow had grown up in Oak Heart. She left after graduation to backpack Europe, and she didn't come back home for more than a decade. Now she'd moved back to raise her daughter.

In Oak Heart, summers are best. The sloping lawn that tumbled toward town from Morris College's stately Stone Hall met up with the city park at the shared band shell and hosted summer concerts nearly every week all summer. An eclectic mix of families, summer college kids, on-break faculty, and townies Frisbeed, hula-hooped, and danced until the sun went down.

Meadow and her friend Natalie were 'walking the loop' on one of the last summer concerts of the year. They followed the meandering path and drank from miniature plastic bottles of wine, which they'd received from a foursome of drunken college boys.

A Frisbee sailed over their heads, close, and a shirtless boy in flip-flops bounded after it, shouting a careless "Sorry, ladies" over his shoulder along with a disarming grin. Meadow and Natalie waved, and Meadow pondered aloud how once upon a time she'd have been able to jump and catch that thing. Natalie asked which thing? And they were still laughing when they came across Mickey.

Mickey was standing with Jessie at the crossroads of two pathways. He was swaying slightly, and laughing that braying laugh of his. Meadow and Natalie stopped short and Mickey greeted them as old friends.

"Well, girls, where are we going now?" he asked.

"I don't know, Mickey, where should we go?" Meadow said.

"There's a Celtic band playing at Neptune's. I think they're Celtic. Blarney Stoned — that'd be Celtic, wouldn't it?"

"You should come," Jessie said, laughing, her eyes bright. "It'll be so much fun."

"I don't know," Natalie said. "How long did your mother say she'd watch the girls?"

"They'll be fine. You should totally come." Jessie had the same pleadingly playful look as a puppy.

"We do have a couple hours yet," Meadow said.

"Yay!" Jessie celebrated.

"So, you're coming? Celtic band? C'mon, let's dance a jig." Mickey broke into a clumsy dance, grabbing Natalie's hand. She jigged with him, laughing.

Jessie shook her head indulgently. "We'll see you there, then."

"Neptune's," she said to a boy as she passed him.

Meadow heard him tell his friends, as they caught up with him, that they should go to Neptune's now. She laughed. Natalie laughed. It was good to be outside on a summer night, drinking wine, laughing with friends, throwing their heads back to see the stars, and feeling their hair swish. It made them feel possibilities they didn't often feel as single moms.

Neptune's was reassuringly unchanged. They beelined for a spot at the bar near Gordon, a mutual friend and Neptune's fixture.

"That doesn't look like a Celtic band to me," Meadow said.

"Is it supposed to be a Celtic band?" Gordon said.

"Mickey told us it was." Natalie pantomimed drinking. "But who knows."

"Jessie with him? Oh, there's going to be some dancing tonight!"

Moments later Jessie herself glided into view. She smiled and waved at Meadow and Natalie, beckoning as she threaded her way to the dance floor. Natalie followed her, but Meadow shook her head.

"I need more beer first," she said.

"I guess that's not a Celtic band," Mickey said, unnecessarily, as the first power chords shattered the room. "Blarney Stoned — sounds Celtic, you know what I mean?"

The night passed as such nights will. Meadow nursed her beer, thinking about work the next day, the drive home, the probability that Natalie would have to crash on the couch. She watched Jessie dance, the red and blue from the neon beer signs warming and cooling her face as she twisted and twined and laughed. And Mickey laughed and talked, everyone in the bar a friend within minutes. He laughed, he lurched, he slurred, he drank shot after shot, beer chasers to every one.

He staggered over to Meadow. "So, you're having fun, right? You got to have fun at Neptune's, you know what I mean?"

Meadow acknowledged she was indeed having fun. Natalie moved on and off the dance floor like a moth against the window.

Mickey turned toward a young man sitting with his friends, watching Jessie. He looked out of place, the young man, as if he didn't venture into bars like Neptune's often. Mickey put his arm around him, talked quietly, and then moved away. The young man suddenly slipped off his bar stool and stood there, his face slack, hanging onto the bar for support, weaving.

"Oh, his head is going to ache tomorrow," Mickey said, returning to Meadow, his eyes merry.

Meadow looked at him sharply. Mickey was standing upright, his eyes clear, no slur to his speech. She would have sworn just minutes ago he was at the fall-down-drunk stage. He winked at her, and she answered him with an uncertain smile.

She watched Mickey as he sauntered over to watch a group of guys shoot pool. He finished the drink in his hand. One of the guys handed him another, and he knocked that one back, his hand already around a third. The guy who'd been at the bar was taking a heckling from his friends.

"You didn't even drink that much, man. Jared's a lightweight," one of them said.

The guy at the bar — Jared, evidently — looked confused as well as drunk. "I know. I was fine, and all of a sudden, wham.

I don't know if I can drive." He was laughing and slurring and wobbly on his feet.

"You can't. Give me your keys, lightweight."

Meadow watched as Jared's friends escorted him from the bar. She glanced at Mickey and saw he was watching them, too, the delighted smile of a mischievous boy on his face. Someone handed him a tequila shot and a beer, and he glanced Meadow's way and toasted her.

Meadow thought back over the night. She didn't typically sit and observe in a bar, being more of an in-the-crowd type most nights. But she had an artist's eye for detail and the memory to go with it. When she and Natalie had arrived, a guy in khaki shorts had been at the front corner of the bar, chatting up a college girl a decade his junior. Meadow remembered seeing Mickey talking with him when he and Jessie had first arrived, and shortly after that, the guy had laid his head on the bar, stupidly smiling, and had been hauled out by a couple of his friends, same as Jared.

"Gordie, you ever notice that Mickey sort of sobers up in a hurry?" she asked.

"What?" Gordon turned on his stool to look at her. He glanced at Mickey. Mickey was leaning against the wall, a stupid smile on his face, talking with the guys near the pool table.

"He's looking pretty drunk now," Gordon observed.

"But not long ago, he wasn't. And before that he was."

"Yeah, yeah, I guess I know what you're talking about. Never really thought about it. You know, a lot of alcoholics can drink a keg's worth and still be functional."

He shrugged, and turned back to watch the dancers.

Natalie appeared out of the crowd, handed Meadow a foam-topped plastic cup, and pirouetted to return to dancing.

Meadow caught her hand for just a minute. "It's almost midnight, Cinderella," she said.

"Should we go?"

"We'll stay a little longer, but pretty soon."

Natalie set her empty cup on the bar.

"You should dance at least one, Meadow."

"You should dance," Mickey said, watching as Natalie answered Jessie's beckoning wave from under the lights. He was standing next to Meadow, where he hadn't been a moment before.

"Oh, I… Not really in the mood. And I drove, so …"

"Those guys think you like me," he said, indicating with his elbow the group by the pool table. "You keep looking at me and talking about me."

"I do like you, Mickey," Meadow said carefully. Mickey was drunk. So drunk she didn't know how she could have thought he was sober.

Meadow looked around her. The long room, pool table to one side, tiny dance floor in back by a small corner stage, the red bar stools. It was all very familiar, and somehow tonight it seemed ominous.

"There's nothing to be afraid of," Mickey said. "Sometimes I just like to show off, you know what I mean? I wouldn't even tell you now, except for that I'm a little drunk."

"Show off what?"

"What I do."

"What do you do, Mickey?"

"You know, most people never notice," he said. "You, though, you pay attention. I borrow sobriety."

Meadow laughed. "What the eff?"

"It's just a matter of picking likely people, you know what I mean? Someone who's been in the bar all night or someone who is dancing a lot or someone who is loud anyway or someone who is alone."

"I don't understand. You borrow sobriety?"

"Well, take it. I more take it then borrow it, because I don't give it back. Or I guess you could say I swap it, you know what I mean?"

Meadow stared hard at Mickey, Mickey who was swaying slightly with drink, his eyes glassy, his smile crooked.

He looked past her to the dance floor, where Jessie twisted and turned and laughed and enchanted.

"Look at my girl, she's a little nymph."

Meadow automatically looked to the dance floor. Jessie's eyes flew open and she waved at Meadow and laughed that delighted laugh of hers.

"So, what are you?" she asked.

"Everybody is all charged up about vampires and werewolves these days, you know what I mean? Those are the celebrities. I'm just a little guy, just doin' my own thing. Guys like me, we've been around a long time, a real long time. Know what I mean?"

Meadow's eyes had gone wide. Mickey smiled, nodding his head. "Ah, you're starting to believe me."

"I have to go. My mom, the girls," she stammered. She turned her head side to side, looking for Natalie. She saw Natalie across the room, edging away from the dancing. Natalie, who never wore a watch, gestured at her wrist to indicate time and raised her eyebrows in a question. She started coming their way.

Mickey stepped close to Meadow. She felt rooted to the spot. "Why did you tell me this?" she said, and she could hear fear in her voice.

Mickey smiled at her. "You probably won't remember it anyway, or you'll think it was just a notion." He seemed to stumble, and he put his arm around Meadow and said something she couldn't understand, as if in another language. For just a moment, she saw Mickey's eyes clear, the slackness leave his face, his posture improve.

And suddenly she was drunk.

"You ready?" Natalie asked her.

"I sure am," Meadow said, throwing her hands into the air and hula dancing in the direction of the dance floor. She bumped her hip against Gordon and laughed helplessly at the look on his face. Jessie beckoned from the dance floor, smiling and laughing.

Natalie stared after Meadow. She turned to Mickey. "She was fine just a second ago. What'd you do to her?"

Mickey laughed, his clear eyes full of mischief.

"Let's dance," he said.

WAKING UP BLACK

Susan Pieters

Sue is a Vancouver-area writer whose most recent contest win is the Cedric Award for memoir. She has a master's degree and has taught English overseas, but she loves being an editor at Pulp Literature because these amazing stories open her mind to new worlds. She hopes this story will do the same for other readers.

Waking Up Black

The bell was loud enough to be heard for miles around. That was my first thought, waking up, wondering what the sound was for. Fire alarm? Nuclear attack? But I was wrong. It was much more serious, and heard much farther away than I realized.

The funny part is what I noticed first. I focused on my bed. Or the lack of bed. I had been sleeping on the floor.

When I stood up, my clothes were all wrong. The room was all wrong. Only then did I see my arms were all wrong.

I thought I was in the shadows. Or covered with mud. Or something.

"What is this?" I cried out. *Cried* is a polite word. I was swearing under my breath and growing more terrified by the second. The alarm bells had stopped, but my legs were quaking.

"It was time to change places." I recognized my husband's voice, but it was muted. He was squatting, his back to me, stirring a pot on a burner. It wasn't even a stove. There was actual smoke coming from the bottom. "Our turn was over."

"What turn?"

"Our turn at being white."

I looked again at my arms. My feet. The back of my husband's legs. "Are we really black?"

His laugh was deep. "We'll get used to it."

"But who decided this? It's not fair."

"Fair? Did you think *fair* was what you were born with?"

I looked at the single square room. It was filled with nothing but junk, bits of things, the useless clutter I kept in the garage before I threw it away or gave it to the thrift store. Bits of old blankets, a beat-up toy, faded paperbacks, a cassette player that had to be twenty years old.

"When do we get to switch back?"

Again he laughed. "Be grateful we have cornmeal for breakfast." His head was bent over his wooden spoon. "And be grateful I was up first to cook it for you."

"Will they help us, do you think?"

"Who?"

"The black people. Now that they're white."

"Why should they?"

"Because we're not used to this. At least they'll understand what we're going through."

The back of his shaved head nodded. "That's an interesting idea."

"It's not like we chose to be born white."

He wrapped his hand around the handle of the pot and stood up, lifting it off the burner. He turned to me. The person I knew as my husband was no longer a man, but a woman. He, I mean she, noticed my shock. "It's not like we chose our sex, either."

I looked down at myself. I was male. It felt normal. I hadn't even noticed.

My husband/wife picked up a large jug. "I'm off to get water. Enjoy being the man for a while."

I sat down on the floor. It was dirt, but hard as cement. "How long will this last?"

I heard the soft chuckle of my husband/wife as they walked down the long road to the well. At least, I hoped it was a well. Their voice was a mix of sadness and hope. "As long as it takes," they said.

INDEBTED

Summer Jewel Keown

Summer Jewel Keown is an Indianapolis native recently transplanted to Ithaca, NY. Her short stories have been printed in HoosierLit *and the upcoming* Bikes In Space, *Vol. 5. She recently had a short play produced by IndyFringe. Follow her on Twitter @TheSummerJewel or visit summerjewelkeown.com.*

$ 44,861. 75

*I*ndebted

Erica stood at the back of the breakfast line, fiddling with her bracelet, trying to decide if she really needed food this morning. Her stomach growled in response and she shook her head, took a tray. The numbers on her bracelet were lit like scarlet letters: $44,845.67.

She took a banana and a cup of runny oatmeal. That should be enough to last her until lunch, she hoped. She reached her arm up to the cashier and heard the familiar beep. The numbers on her bracelet ticked up: $44,849.75. She sighed, looked around the cafeteria.

Shaelyn saw her and stood to wave her over, smiling broadly. Erica couldn't help but smile back. She walked over and slid into the seat across from the closest thing she had to a friend.

"You look nice today," Erica said, noticing Shaelyn's new hoop earrings and her carefully tended curls.

"They're from Alan," Shaelyn whispered conspiratorially.

"Your boss, Alan?" Erica asked, trying to hide the concern in her voice.

"He's really taken an interest in me." Shaelyn brushed an errant strand of hair behind her ear, the fake gold of her own bracelet reflecting the light. Erica tried not to notice the numbers, but couldn't help herself: $225,889.16 glowed brightly. Erica's heart sank. She didn't know how Shaelyn would ever pay that off. No wonder she was looking at other options.

Erica devoured her small breakfast and listened to Shaelyn tell stories about her life from before. They probably never would have met, let alone been friends, though Erica liked to think they could have been, if they'd met. But their worlds simply wouldn't have touched.

Shaelyn said she'd met Leonardo DiCaprio on a yacht once in Cyprus, not that he would probably remember her now. If only, right? Her $225K would be nothing to him. But that was before. Erica imagined the glamour of that world. The parties, the clothes, the gourmet food. She wouldn't trade for it, though, knowing what they all knew now.

Erica was so caught up in Shaelyn's stories that she realized with a start she was going to be late. She excused herself, and Shaelyn pulled her into a tight hug.

"You take care of you," Shaelyn said, like she did every day.

"I always do," Erica replied, like she did every day.

Erica ran to where the transport vehicles were idling outside. A mini bus waited to take her group to the Brookside warehouse, and she rushed to catch it. She scanned her bracelet for the fare ($44,859.75), found an open seat, rested her head against the window, and let her thoughts drift to the before.

Her son had fallen from a tree, the voice on the other end of the phone call had said. They'd rushed him in an ambulance to the nearest hospital, and she could meet him there. Her heart in her throat, the Erica of seven years before had driven as fast as she could without risking being pulled over on the way. Dustin had to be OK, he just had to.

At the hospital, they told her that yes, her son was there. He was OK, he'd just broken his leg, possibly had a concussion. He was going to be fine. And yes, she could see him, but first she needed to fill out some paperwork. She'd begged the woman at the front desk to let her see him first. He was probably scared out of his mind, and he needed his mom. But the woman insisted. It was policy. Erica had filled out the forms so quickly they were barely legible, initialed where the woman pointed, barely reading what she was filling out. She didn't care, she had to get to Dustin, let him know that Mom was here, and he was safe.

Finally, they led her back. Dustin was a little woozy, but was happily watching cartoons on the television. Tears of relief rose to her eyes.

"My baby," she said, throwing her arms around him.

"Moooom," he complained halfheartedly, but she felt him hug her back.

If I ever lost him, she thought, my life would be over.

They'd set his leg and discharged him a few hours later. Dustin begged the nurse pushing his wheelchair to the door to go faster. On the way home he'd bragged about how all his friends at school would sign his cast and it was going to be so cool.

That night, she tucked in her boy and checked back in on him once he fell asleep, watching him breathe in and out and thanking God that he was okay.

It was a month later that the notices started coming in the mail. Bills upon bills, envelopes with large red block-letter print warning her to pay. She tried to work out a payment plan with the hospital, but she couldn't even meet the minimums. The warning letters became more and more threatening, and then the phone calls started. No matter what she tried, she could never pay enough.

Then one day, she got a new letter that said the National Independent Bank had purchased her debt and she was now required to repay them instead. She thought it was strange that someone would want to buy her debt when it was obvious that she couldn't pay it. It didn't make sense. Not until the Act.

The transport bus pulled up outside of the warehouse, and the women shuffled off. Erica followed and walked down the long corridor to her section, the order fulfilment station. She nodded at her boss, an older woman wearing her own gold bracelet. Her boss's number was down to only $700. They would need a new manager soon, and Erica prayed it would be her. She'd been working hard, trying to get faster, more efficient as she pulled books, clothing, cooking supplies for the people who ordered them online. She had even figured out a way to tweak the arrangement of the spice section to make the jars easier to pull and less likely to break as they worked at high speeds.

Who knew where her boss would go when she was all paid off? If she couldn't find a non-bracelet job, she'd probably end up right back here again. Erica had noticed it around the warehouse — workers were thrilled to finally be de-braceleted, but with so much work becoming bracelet work now, almost no one on the outside needed manual labour anymore. The women would borrow again for their rent, their food, try to find any job that would take them. But they ended up back here as often as not, when the banks called in their debt once again.

On her first break of the day, Erica bought a bottle of water ($44,861.75) and at lunch she bought a sandwich from the vending machine ($44,865.25), praying that she wouldn't get food poisoning from the poorly refrigerated unit. She'd given up complaining about the cost of things, about the fact that there was nowhere else to get food so she was stuck with what was offered. Prices were always ticking up. They blamed inflation, of course. She tried to be zen about it, hunker down and get through.

When the bell rang, ending her double shift, Erica stood in line to clock out. She scanned her bracelet and watched the numbers roll back ($44,790.25). Then she got back on the transport vehicle ($44,800.25) and headed back to her housing facility. She scanned in for the night ($44,825.25).

Erica badly wanted to call home. She missed her boy, who was a teenager now, and ached to hear his voice. But phone calls out cost one dollar per minute, so she only allowed herself one short call a week.

Lying on her cot in the cell that they called a dormitory, Erica wondered if her son would know her when she got out. Her heart had broken when her mother wrote her that Dustin wanted to send her his meagre allowance to help pay down her balance. It had broken even more that she'd briefly considered it.

When the Debt Responsibility Act had been proposed, no one had really paid attention. Especially not Erica. Its more vicious provisions had been hidden behind claims of enforcing personal responsibility and protecting the financial solidity of our important institutions, the banks. No one, other than the true policy wonks, realized something unusual was afoot. At least, not until the banks started buying up the private prisons. Until they merged into super-corporations with holdings in manufacturing, shipping, and all manner of operations that might benefit from cheap manual labour.

Truthfully, it was brilliant, in a Machiavellian sort of way. Businesses needed cheap labour, the private prisons needed to fill beds, and the banks wanted to keep people from defaulting on their debts.

By the time people realized what was happening, it was already in motion. Buried deep in the law, in language only a seasoned lawyer could parse, was the provision that allowed debtors to call in their debts at any time. If you could not pay, you were legally considered a thief. And thieves had no right to liberty.

Talk show hosts debated heatedly in the 24-hour news cycle. On one side, critics called it the new debtors' prisons, harkened back to the cruelty of Victorian jails. On the other, proponents castigated those who owed for being freeloaders, mooching off hardworking taxpayers, hindering economic growth, and harming the health of our beloved corporations.

Lawyers tried to free their clients, arguing that owing a corporation was not a jailable offense. But perhaps it was only a matter of time after Citizens United before owing a debt to a company would be no different than mugging another person on the street.

The banks had a brilliant PR campaign designed and ready to roll out the moment public sentiment began turning against them. They blanketed the airwaves, YouTube, Facebook. Talking heads on television, not-so-secretly receiving sponsorships from the banks, vociferously supported them. In a clever marketing strategy, pop star Taylor Swift became the face of taking personal responsibility for your debts, and the millennials begrudgingly fell in line.

It happened slowly at first, the rollout. First they took the people no one would really miss, the men and woman who got out of prison and had to borrow to get by while they looked for more work. They grabbed the working poor using check-cashing services to avoid the banks' steep fees. And then, when it started to become the new normal, they took anyone they wanted.

Not the rich, of course. No matter what sums the rich owed, they were safe. The banks had discretion to call in debts where they declared it necessary for financial solvency. Suspiciously, that meant thousands and then tens of thousands of the poor and middle class. But rarely the wealthy, even when they owed huge sums. Unless one of the wealthy crossed a line, of course. Made waves. Owed the wrong people. Or just fell out of favour. Like Shaelyn.

The banks could buy up debt from anywhere: student loans, missed car payments, back rent, underwater mortgages. Those who owed lived in a constant state of fear, taking on second, even third jobs to push back the threat of the Debt Police.

Erica had taken on extra shifts at the nursing home where she had worked before, but when her mother couldn't watch Dustin, she couldn't afford to find a sitter. She and Dustin moved in with her mother to try and save rent. They had made contingency plans, hoping never to have to use them. Erica had seen the Debt Police in her neighbourhood more than once, rolling up in their shiny black-and-orange vans, banging on someone's front door, breaking it down if it wasn't answered post haste. Erica prayed that she could pay down her debt before they came for her.

The rumour was that if you made payments on your debt above the minimum, you were more profitable to the banks working on the outside than at one of their facilities, in one of their assigned jobs. Erica budgeted harder than she ever had before, finding new ways to season beans and rice, feeding her son before herself, spending as little as she could possibly manage. But life was so expensive that she could barely make ends meet.

And then, they came. They always seemed to come at night. Maybe it was more dramatic that way. Erica wondered sometimes why people took jobs with the Debt Police, spent their days ripping families apart. No matter what it paid, she didn't think she could do it.

It was 2:00 a.m. and the neighbourhood was quiet. That was one possible benefit since the Debt Police began — fewer people out on the street. There was still crime, but there was a price tag attached. Every person arrested was now directly responsible for all associated costs: the salaries of the police officers who arrested them, the photographer at the jail who took their mug shot, the guard who guarded them, the admins who processed their paperwork. They were responsible for the food they ate in jail, their portion of the utilities, and a vague rehabilitation fee. No one could afford those fees, so instead of being released, prisoners were transferred to the repayment facilities until they could work their way free. 'Repayment Facility' was the official name, but most people just called it debt prison.

The Debt Police slammed a fist against the door, standing underneath the motion-sensitive porch light, the light reflecting off shiny black riot helmets. From up in her bedroom, Erica knew it was for her. They had finally come.

They had papers with her face and debt information, held it up to her to ensure they matched.

"Right hand out," one of the identical officers demanded.

"Please," Erica whispered, tears in her eyes. "I'm paying off my debt. I need to be here for my boy."

"I will ask again, only once. Hand. Out." She could not see his eyes through the visor. He could have been anyone underneath.

Erica reached out her hand. The officer held up a golden bracelet, open at the hinge, with numbers embedded in glowing red.

"Erica Holmes, you are in debt to the National Independent Bank for the sum of $75,610.82. Your debt has been recalled. You will be transferred to a repayment facility and assigned work until such time as your debt is repaid. You have the right to an attorney, should you be able to afford one."

The officer placed the bracelet around her wrist and closed it with an audible click.

She was held in a conference room until dawn. It was just her at first; then it started to fill. By the time the sun came up, the room was full. No one spoke to each other. They looked downcast, defeated, staring at the new bracelets that may as well have been handcuffs.

Everyone knew by now what would happen, or at least the gist of it. The repayment facilities were billed as a way to pay off one's debt and re-enter society. But there was a catch. Always a catch. There were no free rides in this brave new world.

After hours of sitting, and waiting, a suited woman strolled in. She had the no-nonsense manners of someone who was not there to make friends. The woman picked up a small remote control and pushed buttons to roll down a screen and turn on a projector. Orientation began.

They were here because they had become a burden to society and their debt threatened the stability of our homeland's economy. This was a crime. But the banks did not wish to imprison them, though they had every right to do so. Instead, the criminals would be afforded the opportunity to work off their debt, and to learn new skills in the process.

Their lodging, food, transportation, and other necessities would be provided at reasonable costs, which would be added to the debt total on their bracelets. Upon completing work each day, their wages would be deducted from the total. When their balance reached zero, they would be free to return home as financially responsible citizens.

Once orientation was completed, she told them, new residents would complete a skills test to determine the best assignment for them moving forward. The cost of this test would, of course, be added to their bracelet.

"Welcome," said the woman, who had never identified herself by name, to the silent group. A woman in the back cried quietly. "We wish you all the best in your repayment journey."

That had been seven years ago. Erica had tested into the sorting and shipping section at the warehouse. She soon learned that it was easy to end up in more debt by the end of the day, once food, transportation, and necessities like soap, tampons, and toothpaste were added on. Erica had tested her limits, trying to eat as little as possible, until the day she collapsed at work. They had nearly called for a medic, but luckily a coworker had propped her up and helped her fulfil her orders for the day. If the medic had come, the cost would have taken her another year to pay down.

Her first night in the facility, Erica cried for hours. She didn't know if she would ever see her son again, if her mother would be all right in her absence, if she would ever again be free. She knew to keep quiet. If a guard were called, a five-dollar fee would be assessed. The first day's fees had already added weeks to her repayment plan. She stuffed her scratchy blanket (for which they had billed her $20) into her mouth to blot out the sound.

"Psst," she heard from the cell next to her, the sound seemingly coming from a grate on the adjoining wall. She ignored it at first.

"Hey," the voice said. "You're going to get through this. I promise."

It was Shaelyn.

Erica had responded to her politely at first, not wanting to make herself at home. That made it seem too real. She wanted to just go through the motions, keep her head down. Spend as little as possible, take on as many shifts and as many hours at the warehouse as they would allow her. But slowly, Shaelyn became someone she looked forward to seeing in the morning at breakfast and hearing at night before she went to sleep.

Erica wasn't sure how she stayed so upbeat and positive. Shaelyn treated this whole experience like it was just another adventure. She had tested into a position answering phones at a law firm—one of the integrated positions, new-ish to the program, where the indebted worked alongside the free. She seemed to love it, coming back each day with tales of the moneyed lawyers she assisted.

"How was Alan today?" Erica asked as they brushed their teeth together. "Did he offer to pay off your debt and whisk you away to Aruba?"

"You laugh," Shaelyn said with an impish smile, "but I think he's about to ask me."

It was not unheard of for the indebted to marry those who could pay off their debt. The banks didn't really care how they got their money, after all. They were happy to let a husband pay off his new wife's debt. But it could also be scary. If they divorced, the husband could levy the debt right back on to his now ex-wife. It meant almost certain re-imprisonment. And so the indebted wives would do anything to keep that from happening, endure any ill-treatment, become servants to their new masters. Some said that it was better than being in the debt prisons regardless, that at least they weren't adding to their debt total and could sleep on comfortable sheets in the meantime.

"I know what you're thinking," Shaelyn said. "You don't need to worry."

"Do you … really want to be married to him?" Erica asked.

Shaelyn's smile faltered for a moment, then corrected itself. "Of course. He's a good man. And …" She held up her bracelet, its many digits glowing red inside the gold.

Erica had no room to judge, she knew. Shaelyn's number meant she would likely never be free again, or at least not until she was so old that she would never find work on her own. Erica didn't know what she would do in that situation.

"I hope that everything goes exactly as you want it to." Erica smiled and hoped that it looked sincere. She didn't know what she hoped for Shaelyn. They both wanted the same thing: to be free. Marriage just wasn't an option Erica had to consider.

Even if there were a man she could marry, she wouldn't risk that life with her son.

They said their good-nights and went back to their dorms. Sometimes the women would whisper between their cells until they fell asleep, but tonight they were silent. Erica assumed that Shaelyn was deep in thought, considering what she would do next — if she would accept Alan's offer, if he made it.

The next morning, Erica got herself ready and went to the cafeteria as usual. She got her banana and oatmeal ($44,8923.33). She went to sit at their usual table, but Shaelyn wasn't there. That was odd, Erica thought. Shaelyn was always on time. Maybe she had been up late dreaming of her new life, and she'd overslept.

She sat there, delaying, until a few minutes before the transport was due to leave. If this was the day that Alan popped the question, she wanted to see Shaelyn off beforehand and make sure she knew that she still had a choice, even if it didn't seem like one. But her friend did not come to join her.

The hand on the clock shifted on the wall. She had to go. She couldn't afford to miss a day of work, and if she missed the transport bus, she would have to pay out of pocket for a solo shuttle, wiping out her entire day's pay. Erica stood, resigned, and started to make her way to the transports.

An alarm rang out. Loud, shrill, deafening. The women here were so well-behaved, afraid to be fined, that the alarm was rarely needed, and its sound was shocking. In the hall, Erica saw people running toward her cell. Toward Shaelyn's cell.

"No," she whispered to herself, fear leaping up into her throat. She found herself walking back toward her cell in the opposite direction from the transports. There was a crowd already huddled around Shaelyn's cell as she neared. She could feel tears building into a ball in her chest.

"Get back," someone yelled at the gathering crowd. The crowd pretended not to hear. Erica pushed her way to the front. The other women let her. They knew she was Shaelyn's friend.

She could barely see at first, blocked by guards' bodies. Then someone in the crowd whispered: *That's why they shouldn't allow pantyhose.*

Oh god, no. Erica made eye contact with a guard, who gave her the tight smile of someone who wants to be anywhere else. She dropped her eyes and noticed the gold bracelet on the guard's own arm. The guard's eyes now averted, Erica turned her head to Shaelyn's bed.

They had cut her down, laid her on the bed, covered her with a sheet. But her arm hung down toward the floor. The right one. The gold-coloured bangle bracelet hung limply on her wrist, its red numbers still glowing.

Erica felt nothing for a moment. And then she ran. She got to the bathroom just in time to be sick into the cold porcelain bowl. She retched, and cried, one after the other, until she was empty.

She should have known. She should have realized that Shaelyn didn't want that golden ticket out, but that she couldn't stay here. She should have heard something, anything, last night, instead of sleeping like the dead.

When she calmed, Erica sat up. She washed her face and looked at herself in the mirror: skin wan, eyes red.

She went out to the hall and paused. There was nothing she could do now. She walked out of the building to the transport vehicles. The buses were gone, of course. They were nothing if not punctual. A single taxi sat there. "Bracelet payments accepted," it said in small print on the side.

She opened the door, slipped into the backseat, and held out her arm to be scanned. The driver glanced back at her.

"I heard what happened in there," he said. "I'm sorry to hear it."

Erica nodded. She couldn't speak for fear of sobbing. She pushed her bracelet toward him, nodding at his scanner.

"Brookside Warehouse," she whispered, her voice cracking.

"Put that away," he said. "This is not a day for that."

She rode in silence with the kind taxi cab driver, on her way to pay her debts.

ALPHABET SOUP

Alex Reece Abbott

Alex Reece Abbott has racked up an impressive list of awards in recent years and is clearly a fiction writer to watch. Currently writing primarily in short fiction, Alex has been a finalist for the Tillie Olsen Prize, Maria Edgeworth Short Fiction Prize, Sunday Business Post/Penguin Ireland Short Story Prize, and Bath Novella-in-Flash Prize and her stories have won the HG Wells Grand Prize, the Northern Crime Prize, and Crediton Short Story Prize. Her novel, The Helpmeet, is a Greenbean Irish Novel Fair winner. This gem of flash fiction was shortlisted for Pulp Literature's Hummingbird Prize, judged by Bob Thurber. You can find out more about Alex at alexreeceabbott. info or on Twitter @AlexReeceAbbott.

${\mathcal{A}}$LPHABET SOUP

She's making changes, taking risks, heading in a new direction.

You want to be supportive. It's important you stay cool and mask any surprise. Hide your tailspin. No one has all the answers.

You coddle and fuss, a fellow passenger on her mood roller coaster, a constant companion through long nights of tears and talk, shames and shoulda-beens. She grumbles at your smothering, confesses the confusion and doubt have been with her for years.

You rake at memories, scanning her childhood for warnings and nascent realisations, all the signals you ignored or missed. How could you see this coming? How could any mother. You curse those who told you it was just a phase.

You investigate health insurance, trying to wrap your head around the path she's on. The lack of local professional support eats at you.

You worry over pronouns, kicking yourself after each fumbling. When you're alone, you practise, rehearsing in whispers, rewiring your brain. You watch her segueing. Looking at old photographs, memory and sentiment crest. She never grew out of it.

Turns out, genes are complicated, more subtle than we knew. They follow no simple linear pattern. The ache of deprivation and absence jostle with who you may gain from this chromosomal mix-up. You work out how much of a life you can have with all the years of consultations, analysis. The treatments and surgeries. The stigma.

Clearly there's no right way, no magic wand you can wave to make things easier as she reaches for her essence and struggles to claim her place. You can't lose her. No mother is ever prepared for that. You take an oath, determined to show love—constant, simple, beyond any alphabet soup. You help her find the right bra, the right make-up, the right walk, the right smile. You offer her a uterus. You are making changes, fresh choices, taking a new direction. It's your transition too.

THE HUB

Erin Evans

Erin Evans *grew up on the West Coast of Canada and has worked as a high school English and Creative Writing teacher for the past 18 years. She is passionate about her two children, husband, creative projects, bookstores, tea, and good food. 'The Hub' is a story that snuck up on her, and it is her first publication credit, as it garnered an honourable mention from Jack Whyte and Diana Gabaldon at the Surrey International Writers' Conference in 2017.*

The Hub

The street is impenetrable with tourists, shoppers, and locals all pushing past each other to get somewhere, anywhere, as long as they keep moving. It is a sea of movement and as close to the ocean as this little town will ever get.

We opened the shop nine days ago. We tell them that we are a front for several sting operations and not a real café, but they keep coming. We sell drinks for unreasonable prices, but they keep coming. We give incorrect change, but they keep coming. Every day we remove one chair, but they keep coming, sitting on window ledges and leaning on counters. They need somewhere to be and they don't complain. There is consistent chatter. A continuous buzz.

We sell coffee. Weak. Strong. No one notices. Our slogan is 'Drinks and Dreams at Unreasonable Prices'. No one comments. Maybe they think the dream part is simply a bit of whimsy and the unreasonable prices a comical irony. If they are angry or frustrated, they don't show it. They talk on and on and order coffee after coffee. It keeps their hands busy.

On the first day, a patron calls out my name when he orders his coffee. "Antoine, coffee for me and my friends." I smile and think there is a glimmer of something there, but nothing after that first day. Most grunt, and we know what they mean. I'm in daily contact with the boss to report how things are going so far. He is not on site but likes to keep a tight rein on things.

It is amazing how life can change in a moment. Just when I was starting to lose hope, a slip of sweetness floats in and alights on a counter stool like a sparrow on a branch. Her eyes are bright as she searches out every inch of the café, as if challenging its very existence here on this dusty street. Her curiosity has pulled her in and the promise of dreams has made her bold, even in her innocence.

When I have a chance, I ask her what I can get her, and without hesitation she declares, "I'd like a pair of red leather shoes in just my size, please. One strap with a button, oh, and no scuffs, rips, or pinchy edges." The last part she utters with a wink and a grin. I pause as if to say, "We don't do that here," but she knows better and props up her head with her hands and elbows on the counter, ready for my next move. "I had a feeling about you," I divulge. She giggles and kicks her legs against the counter, unable to be still.

I take my time and with an air of grandeur, as best as I can muster, I reach under the counter and come up empty-handed. She frowns just a touch, but her eyes never lose their spark, not even for a moment. I feign confusion and tell her I just need to go downstairs to get them and do the old walking-down-the-stairs-behind-the-counter-trick. Her hands fly to her mouth as she relishes my theatrics. I rise to stand in front of her again and then, in my most serious approach, I produce a plain brown paper-wrapped box on the counter in front of her. I keep one hand on the box, and with the other, I point at our sign: 'Drinks and Dreams at Unreasonable Prices'.

I clear my throat, lean in, and softly state, "Before I hand them over, I must make sure you know the price." She solemnly nods. I slide the box across the short distance between us. As she places her hands on the box, she moves to speak, but I interrupt. "Let's settle payment later. It's busy in here just now, and I know you're good for it. I have an eye for these things, and you are nothing if not trustworthy." I leave her to the box as I serve the masses, all the while sneaking glances at her over my shoulder.

The air around her is electric. A palpable charge. She takes her time opening the box, not quite trusting that her dream shoes could be in there. And as the veil of tissue is lifted, she gasps. It is almost enough to gain a look or a murmur from the other patrons — almost. I, alone, know her joy. It is always a delight to be a part of that moment. Before I know it, her feet have filled the shoes as only her feet can, and she is dancing her way through the café with nary a care in the world, leading with confidence on the best day of her life. I resist the urge to pump my fist in the air. The coffee won't make or serve itself, so I labour on.

The boss is thrilled. We talk late into the night, and he admits his worry about our recent dry spell but, as always, is ever hopeful. His encouragement is clear. "Be ready for anything! Anticipate and deliver … it is the only way." I start today with renewed vigour. It's not long before our little bird reappears. I can practically see the shine of her red shoes coming down the street.

In she floats, barely resting on the edge of her stool. She is giddy and giggly and full of zest for life. She leans back and spins with her dream shoes on display. She doesn't notice that no one notices. She doesn't do it for them anyway. Her joy is striking, to me at least. "What a glorious day! Has it been busy? Anything exciting happen today? What else have people asked you for?" she breathes without really waiting for answers. We laugh easily together at her questions. After a brief silence, she tests the water. "If I were to ask for something else, would that be allowed?" A question she's likely been pondering to herself frequently in the last twenty-four hours, with some worry. She twists her fingers as she waits for my response.

"My dear, for you, a paying customer? Of course you can order more than just one thing."

"But I haven't paid yet," she says carefully.

"I'm certainly not worried about you skipping town," I say, as I playfully gesture to the door. "Skipping through town, yes, but skipping town, no."

I pass her a glass of water, "on the house," give her my best smile, and then work the floor. I fill cup after cup with barely a please or a thank-you. This is how it is. I'm used to it. It is my job and it is packed today. I top up the sugar and the cream. I go back for two more pots, and Red Shoes visualizes her next purchase with daydreamy eyes. Her hands dance up and down the water glass as she hums a little tune. She is a whimsical little one.

"Okay, okay, okay, okay, I'm ready," she starts. "I'd like a basket of freshly baked chocolate chip cookies, please. The kind that melt in your mouth, have at least three chips in every bite, and make you happy to be alive." Her hands fly up to her mouth as if she has spoken out of turn and might want to take those words back. She holds her breath and watches me.

"Fresh ones? A basketful? That is a tall order. Hmm … let me see if I can handle that." And as I send a wink her way, I pop into the back. After a minute, I peek out. She's still kind of frozen in place. I clear my throat, push the door open, and make my way back to her. She slowly drops her hands, and I present her with the cookies. She is stunned, but I can see that her wheels are turning.

She offers me the first cookie. It smells divine and I'm not above gifts, it is a bit of a job perk. We clink our cookies and I say, "Cheers," and offer her a cold glass of milk from below the counter. "It only seems fitting that you enjoy this as well," I say. "Take your time. I have a few guests who need more coffee." She happily settles in with her milk and cookies. I don't ask questions, it is not my place. I simply provide what is asked for.

Each day for a week, she has a new request, and we meet it. Every. Single. Time. I'm doing my job. The boss is so happy with how it is going. "The key is curiosity!" he tells me. "I know I can count on you. Keep up the good work." He calls me first before I can call him, before I can even get the doors closed in the evening. We can both feel that the tide is turning. It is an exciting time. We are on the cusp of change.

Today, for the first time since she came in so many days ago, she looks around. "Is it always this busy in here?"

"Every day. All day," I sing.

"Where do they all come from?" she wonders aloud without intending to.

"Here, there, everywhere. They love our house blend. I can't tell you how many refills I do in a day, per customer. Business is, well, busy." I grin.

She turns towards me after surveying the crowd again. I'm at the ready for her next request. She opens her mouth with that twinkle in her eye but stops, turns back to the hustle and bustle of the café, and is quiet. She rubs her feet together. Freshly polished. "I love it here. What an amazing place this is!" she gushes. She chooses to people-watch today with a salted caramel sundae with the freshest whipped cream, chocolate drizzle, and a cherry on top. This girl is all plume and spiral.

Our little establishment has become part of her daily ritual. We expect to see her now. Her creativity and imagination keep her coming up with the most delightful things. I have never faltered in my delivery. We are always prepared, and that is our promise.

"Today, I want to shake things up a bit," she provokes.

"Oh, really." I bluff shock and then settle into my signature toothy grin. "What'll it be today?" I pull out my order pad and wet my pen on my tongue in anticipation. This is all part of the service.

"I'd like ... what they're having," she says, with a gesture to the crowd.

"No, I don't think so. That's not for you." I laugh. "You aren't serious. What do you really want?"

"No, really I do, Antoine." She looks at the sign. "I want the house blend." She cocks her head to one side, imploring me to consider this seriously, as I have all her previous requests.

"But it is so boring, my dear. Completely beneath you and without zeal."

"I've never had one before. I'd like to try. Do I use milk or sugar? What is the most common?"

So today, our little bird has coffee with lots of milk and sugar. It is something new to add to her growing list. She likes it. I know, because she spins around on her stool and when it is time to go, she hums all the way to the door.

Tonight, the boss says, "Tread carefully."

She dances in the next day and weaves her way through the crowd, hello-ing this way and that to no response from my daily patrons. Not a look, not a grunt, nothing. She sashays up to her regular spot and orders a coffee with a direct look in her eye that says, "Don't even try to persuade me otherwise." So I comply with ease and stay on as a listening ear. She focuses on getting the milk and sugar just right and seems to take pleasure in watching the colour change from black to that creamy flourish of café au lait.

A little splash escapes her cup as she stirs and drops on her red shoes. I quickly grab a cloth for her, but she waves my hand away in a not-to-worry-it's-no-big-deal kind of way, as people do when they don't want to be a bother. I put the cloth down and refill where she has lost a little volume. "Thanks, Antoine, you're the best. I'm so glad I found this place," she says as her eyes survey the room before setting down on the mug again.

"What do they talk about all day, at their tables?" she ponders.

"I'm not sure." And I'm really not. I don't get that involved unless my special skills are required.

"Tomorrow, I'm going to waltz right up to one of their tables and join them."

"You wouldn't dare!" I laugh.

"Mark my words. It's on." She snorts. Then she giggles at her snort, and we both enjoy the moment.

The next day she does just as she said she would. I try to play it cool. I notice her shoes are dull. I see traces of yesterday's mishap. What is my next move? I panic and call the boss. He simply says, "Curiosity and comfort." I'm back on my feet in moments. I tread lightly with coffee to my regulars and bring out a special pot of fresh brew for our girl. She acknowledges me with her best smile but doesn't breach the chatter at her table. She seems very engaged, so I leave her be. I'm run off my feet today, and I miss saying goodbye when I see her signature reds slip out the door.

The sun is just starting to filter in through the front window. It is almost time to open. I watch as the dust plays in the sunbeams and enjoy a quiet moment. It would be a perfect day to fly a rainbow kite across the sky or dig into a fourteen-layer chocolate cake with buttercream icing or be nose to nose with a sweet, darling little kitten, but I know I will have no such requests today. That quiet moment of reflection disappears as the door bangs open and the masses fill the café. In a matter of minutes we are full and (I make sure) so are their cups. I am nothing if not a perfectionist when it comes to my job.

It takes me a moment to spot her but there she is, she has indeed slipped in with the rest of them and taken no notice of me. She is barely noticeable herself. Her shoes are no longer polished, her eyes are no longer animated, and her smile is barely a curve. I try to catch her eye and 'accidently' bump into her, but nothing. I carry on with my usual routine. I will give it a few days, but I know it is time to call in the boss. He needs to see. He's been waiting for my call and tells me he'll be in by the end of the week. He agrees that a little time is important in these matters and applauds my pragmatism.

Today is the day. I get in early to make sure the coffee tanks are full for opening, and the boss is already waiting for me on one of the stools. We nod a greeting and I make sure all is prepared for the day. When things are set, I join him at the counter.

"You've done well here, Antoine." I try not to beam too much at the compliment. Before I can respond, the door opens and scores flood in. The boss watches carefully, for her. I'm already on the floor filling cups.

"I can't pick her out," the boss says when I'm back. "Which one is she?"

I scan the room and wonder if she hasn't come in yet today. Suddenly, it feels very stuffy in here. The boss is waiting, and she's been here every day, but now I'm starting to panic. Face after face just blends in with the next, and then I see her. She is here! She blends in seamlessly with the others. Her red shoes are nearly brown now, but it is, indeed, her. She leans into her cup and drinks. I nearly clap my hands.

"She is there," I start, "at the third table, back to the window, cup in her hands. She is there."

"Ah, yes, I see her. How wonderful, Antoine! She was the last of them here. You've really done a superior job."

"Thank you, sir."

"I'll be in touch once we're ready for you again."

We've cleaned this town of dreamers. It is time to move on to the next and continue what we are tasked with. It takes less and less time now, but we still find pockets of them here and there. The boss says that it really makes the world run so much more smoothly when there is no dissidence. It took years to find the right solution.

It's time to finish the job. I wander over to the third table by the window and lean over to let her know I'm here to collect payment. I ask her if there's anything else I can get her, anything at all. She pays me no heed and simply raises an empty cup.

Her bill is paid in full.

SiWC 2018
October 19-21
+ master classes Oct 18

@SiWCtweets

registration opens on **June 6, 2018**
www.siwc.ca for details

MEAT

Mel Anastasiou

Mel Anastasiou *draws her inspiration for the world of Meat the gargoyle from Pre-Raphaelite canvases and stained glass windows. She is in-house illustrator for* Pulp Literature *and also writes the* Fairmount Manor Mysteries, *starring Stella Ryman, which was long listed for the 2018 Stephen Leacock Memorial Medal for Humour. You can follow her at melanastasiou.wordpress.com*

CALL ME MEAT
THOUGH I'M MADE OF STONE.
I WATCHED WHILE THE OLD KING DIED.
I SAW HIS COUSIN FROM A NEARBY REALM
TAKE THE KING'S DAUGHTER'S HAND.
I PERCHED OUTSIDE.
THE PRINCESS DROPPED THE OLD KING'S CROWN...
IT HOOKED ON MY EAR.
WON'T YOU KEEP IT SAFE FOR ME?
I WILL KEEP IT.
THE NEW KING ANNEXED HER COUNTRY,
AND LOCKED THE CASTLE DOOR.

I POURED RAIN THROUGH MY OPEN MOUTH-
WEARING THE KING'S CROWN, BUT A SLAVE TO THE WEATHER.
I CURSED IT.
LIGHTING STRUCK,
AND CAST ME TO THE GROUND.
I WAS FREE.
TRULY FREE, FOR IN MY CASTLE THERE WERE
NO SOLDIERS TO PAY, NO COURTIERS TO FLATTER.

I MADE GARGOYLES CHANNEL RAIN, THE CASTLE CRUMBLE,
UNTIL THE KING'S DAUGHTER RETURNED ALONE FROM HER COUSIN'S COUNTRY, WITH HER BEDROLL ON HER BACK. SHE KNOCKED AT THE CASTLE DOOR.
I TOLD THE SILENCE,
DON'T ANSWER.
SILENCE DID AS I SAID.
BUT SHE HEARD ME.
I PRUDENTLY HID THE CROWN.
I LUMBERED INTO HER VIEW,
COME OUT, I KNOW YOU ARE THERE.
MY NAME IS MEAT.

MEAT? BUT YOU ARE STONE, LIKE MY CASTLE.
MY CASTLE.
I COULD HAVE KILLED HER THEN, FALLEN FROM ABOVE, SMASHED HER UNDER THE WEIGHT OF MY STONE LIMBS. BUT SHE HAD SOMETHING I CRAVED, A CONFIDENCE I KNEW I HAD TO LEARN I WAS STONE AND WANTED TO BE KING, SO,
PRINCESS, I'LL BE YOUR FIRST MINISTER.
BUT NOT MY LAST. I'VE SENT FOR LOYAL MEN AND WOMEN TO APPROACH MY CASTLE.
MY CASTLE.
SHE LIFTED A VINE, PUSHED AT THE DOOR BEYOND.
SHE FOUND THE THRONE ROOM.

SHE SAT.
CALL ME MAJESTY.
I CALLED HER NOTHING.
BUT I WORKED, AND, GIVE HER DUE,
SHE TOILED AS HARD AS I.
BROKE STONE WITH HER GREAT MALLET,
CLEAREDTHE HALL OF RUBBLE,
SWINGING IT HARD OVER HER SHOULDER.

MY PEOPLE WILL COME SOON, AND CALL ME QUEEN AND RULER.
I SAID NOTHING, EVEN WHEN
SHE FOUND THE CROWN.
SIR MEAT, YOU KEPT IT SAFE FOR ME.
I KEPT IT.
I NEARLY KILLED HER THEN. HER PEOPLE CAME, GATHERED IN THE HALL, EXTOLLED HER. SOLDIERS MARCHED.
I AM MADE OF STONE, BUT I AM NOT STUPID. I COULD SEE MY FUTURE BENEFIT IN HER HARD WORK, GETTING ME SOLDIERS TO PAY, AND COURTIERS TO FLATTER ME. I'D TAKE HER CROWN LIKE HER COUSIN DID, WHEN SHE WAS LITTLE.

WE STOOD ON A PARAPET.
SEE, YOU HAVE TAKEN BACK YOUR COUNTRY.
TRUE. BUT NOW WHAT?
YOU ARE QUEEN.
INDEED, AND WILL HAVE TO KILL MY COUSIN.
YOU CAN DO IT.
I PUSHED BACK MY PLANS TO KILL HER, UNTIL SHE'D WON THE WAR, AND SECURED THE REALM FOR ME.
I AM MEAT, AND I AM MADE OF STONE, BUT I AM NOT AT ALL STUPID.

BUT IN HER SILENCE SHE APPEARED UNSURE.
IT'S YOUR RIGHT TO RULE.
AND MINE TO RULE AFTER YOU.
ALAS, MY COUSIN KING WAS ALWAYS KIND. HE TOOK ME IN.
YOU'RE RIGHT, HE TOOK YOU IN. TOOK YOUR KINGDOM, AS WELL.
QUIET, MEAT. HE RULES WEL HE IS ALWAY TIRED FROM THE WORK.
WILL I RULE A WELL AS HE
ATTACK HIM. YOU'VE SOLDIERS, AND I'LL HELP.
YOU GOOD OLD MINISTE MEAT. I MUST THIN
SHE THOUGHT, ALONE, FOR THREE DAYS AND NIGHTS, WHILE HER MEN AND WOMEN WONDERED WHAT SHE DID.

I BROUGHT A NOTE FROM HER:
Wait for me, loyal folk.
Arm yourselves for war.
SHE'D SAID NO SUCH THING.
BUT HER PEOPLE LISTENED
AND ARMED THEMSELVES FOR WAR.
THEN I KNEW PRECISELY HOW A GARGOYLE COULD RULE,
MAKING STATEMENTS LIKE THIS FROM AN EMPTY THRONE.
SO I WENT TO KILL HER.
THIS WAS NOT AS EASY AS SIX WORDS SOUND.
I'D GROWN FOND OF HER,
ALTHOUGH SHE TOOK MY CROWN.
I CREPT INTO HER CHAMBER.

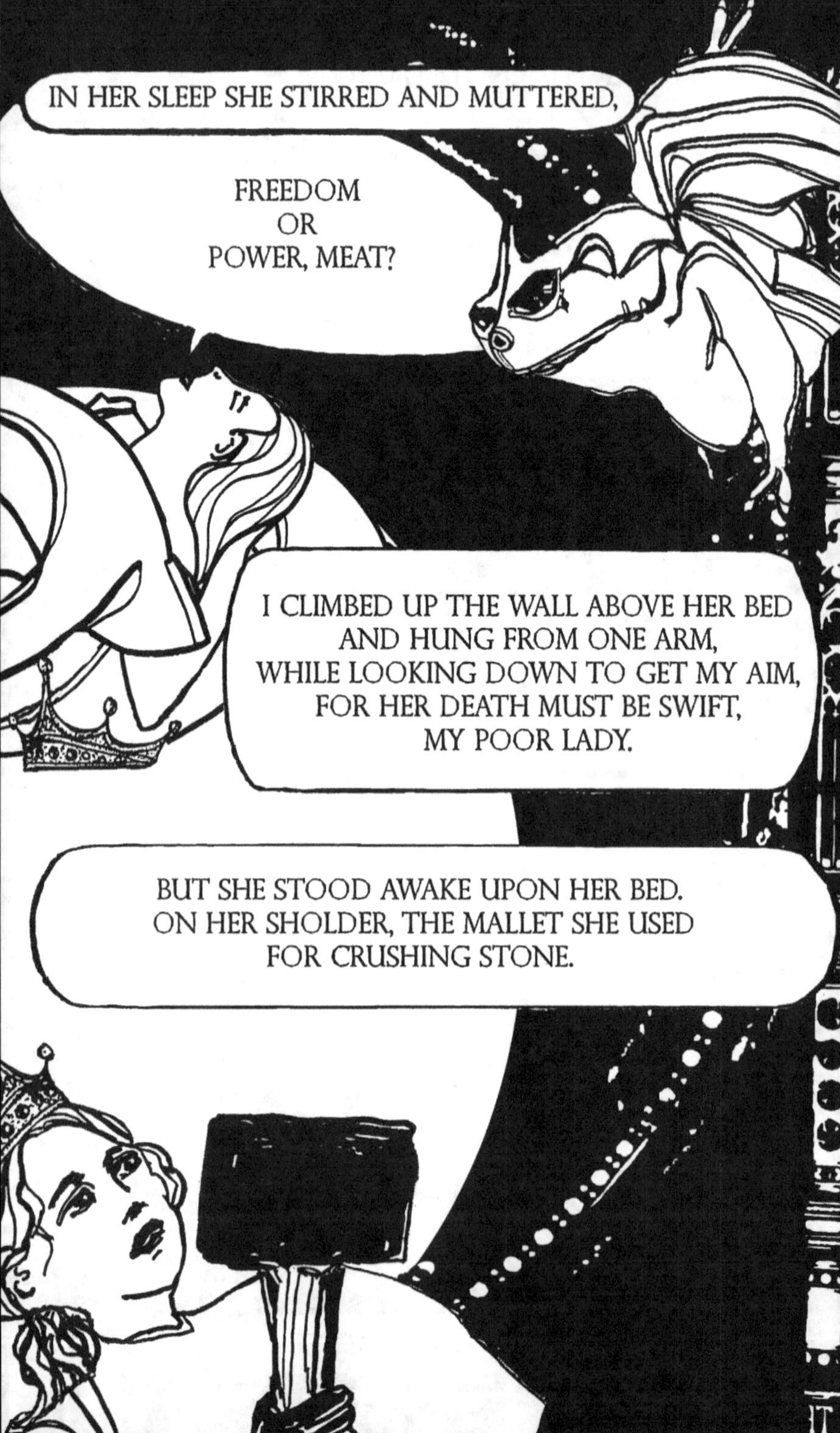
IN HER SLEEP SHE STIRRED AND MUTTERED,
FREEDOM
OR
POWER, MEAT?
I CLIMBED UP THE WALL ABOVE HER BED
AND HUNG FROM ONE ARM,
WHILE LOOKING DOWN TO GET MY AIM,
FOR HER DEATH MUST BE SWIFT,
MY POOR LADY.
BUT SHE STOOD AWAKE UPON HER BED.
ON HER SHOLDER, THE MALLET SHE USED
FOR CRUSHING STONE.

I FELL, WE FOUGHT.
SHE SLUNG HER HAMMER.
I CAST MY STONE LIMBS AT HER AND NEARLY BROKE HER.
SHE NEARLY BROKE ME.
WE BOTH BREATHED HEAVY.
WHAT, MEAT? ARE WE NOT FRIENDS?
LADY, DOES A FRIEND KEEP A MALLET BENEATH HER BED?

WELL, MEAT, I'M YOUNG AND AND MADE OF FLESH, BUT I'M NOT STUPID.
I SAW HOW YOU LOOKED AT MY CROWN.
SHE TOOK THE CROWN OFF. WE STUDIED IT.
SHE TOSSED IT TO ME.
MEAT, KEEP IT.
WHAT, KEEP IT SAFE FOR YOU?
NO, YOU JUST KEEP IT.
BUT, SOLDIERS TO PAY? AND COURTIERS TO FLATTER...
YOU CAN HAVE THEM I CAN'T EVEN KEEP MY FIRST MINISTER LOYAL.
I CAN'T EVEN KEEP MY BEST FRIEND.
SHE ROLLED HER BED AND SLUNG IT ON HER BACK.

FREEDOM OR POWER? I CHOOSE FREEDOM.
I THINK I'LL SEE THE WORLD.
MEAT, GOOD LUCK. YOU'LL NEED IT.
I HELPED HER CLAMBER OUT THE WINDOW, THE SAME WINDOW OUTSIDE WHICH, I, ATTACHED TO STONE, WISHED FOR FREEDOM. NOW I WATCHED HER MAKE HER WAY FROM THE CASTLE GATE.
SO NOW MEN AND WOMEN AWAITED MY ORDERS, AS IF FROM HER. MY LADY CHOSE FREEDOM OVER POWER. NOW, POWER'D CHOSEN ME.
BUT I WISHED TO CHOOSE, NOT BE CHOSEN.
SO, THE SOLDIERS AND COURTIERS WOULD HAVE TO MAKE DO WITH THE COUSIN KING, AND PEACE IN THE KINGDOM. I FOLLOWED HER OUT THE WINDOW, AND BROUGHT THE CROWN ALONG WITH ME.

...BECAUSE SHE'S MORE LIKELY TO CALL ME FRIEND AGAIN, AND TAKE ME INTO THE WORLD, IF I CAN FIND SOMEONE TO MELT THIS CROWN INTO COIN, AND BAG THE JEWELS, TO HIRE US HORSES AND SHIPS ALONG OUR WAY OUT INTO THE GREAT WORLD.
SHE IS FLESH. I AM MEAT.
AND WE'RE LONG GONE FROM THE REALM.

ALLAIGNA'S SONG: ARIA

JM Landels

Allaigna's Song: Aria *is the second novel in the Allaigna's Song trilogy by equestrian swordswoman, artist, and editor* **JM Landels**. *The first book,* Overture, *is available from Pulp Literature Press. You can follow JM's adventures with pen and sword at jmlandels.stiffbunnies.com.*

$\mathscr{P}$REVIOUSLY IN ALLAIGNA'S SONG ...

Fleeing an unwanted betrothal and enraged by her family's lies concerning her parenthood, fourteen-year-old Allaigna has set off to find her true father. However, her quest is interrupted a mere three days by a chance encounter with her betrothed-to-be, Tiern Doniver. When a drunken Doniver decides to claim his promised bride, Allaigna's ability to create magic from music takes a deadly turn, killing her captor. On the road with her new-found mentor Morran Rhoan, Allaigna uses the magic of her voice to disguise herself.

VERSE 15
Running

The road was busy, merchants and other travellers having also delayed their journeys for the weather. Many of the wagons streaming from inns and hostels were headed for the port. An equal number, laden with Aerach wool, barley, wheat and sugar or with finished goods like whisky, porcelain, copper and tin-ware were setting their drays toward eastern Brandishear. Towns there were too far from seaports to acquire goods easily, and were more than happy to put gold and silver into the hands of those traders willing to cross the Sandhorn.

The four-oxen teams were wide and lumbering, and we rode past them where the muddy verges of the road allowed, but all around was cultivated farmland in which we dared not ride in the face of farmers out sowing their crops. When we finally passed the last of the caravans the morning was already gone, but the road was clear and straight ahead of us, with no traffic in sight. I let my voice fall silent at last, taking a long swig from the water-skin that hung from my pommel. I should have been exhausted from my morning of singing, and there certainly was fatigue in my throat and a vague headache threatening. But I was also taken by the beautiful spring day: the intense blue of the sky, the pale green of the newly leafing trees and fields around us, and the clear and flat road ahead.

I looked across at Rhoan. "Race you to that tree," I challenged, pointing to a loan oak at least two furlongs away.

Rhoan's middle-aged eyes crinkled into pure boyishness. Without even a breath to ponder, he kicked Talwis and sent her springing forward in a startled scramble.

I was launched backward and hit the cantle as Nag burst after her. The half-dozen strides in which I slewed in the saddle, regaining my seat and reins, gave Rhoan and his mare a sizeable lead. But though Nag wasn't one of the fine-boned coursers my mother bred, he was long-legged and deep-chested. He stretched his jug head forward and his body dropped beneath me as he flattened into a ground-eating gallop.

Rhoan's mare was fast too, with a densely muscled rump built for comfortable collection at the walk or trot and good for powerful bursts of speed in the short distance. Nag was gaining on her slowly, but he'd never catch her in the distance left between us and the tree.

I sat up straighter. No need to spend my horse completely in a friendly and unwinnable race. As I raised my eyes and eased his pace I caught sight of a glint on the horizon: a flash that was neither water nor glass but the unmistakable flicker of sunlight on steel.

I yelled at Rhoan, urging him to stop, and hauled on Nag's none-too-soft mouth. Rhoan didn't hear me. His form stayed bent over his horse's neck as she kicked up rounds of half-dry mud.

Nag fought me, leaping sideways and giving a crow-hop of

protest, his neck twisting and jaw gaping, incensed at being left behind.

Finally Rhoan looked over his shoulder to see how far ahead he was. He pulled the mare up when he spotted me spinning Nag on the spot. Talwis dutifully rolled back on her haunches and returned to us in her floating trot, ears pricked, pleased with herself after the exhilarating gallop.

At Rhoan's puzzled look, I took a hand off my reins long enough to point at the flash of helmets and armour on the horizon.

"You don't want to run straight into a patrol, do you?"

He shaded his eyes and peered down the road. "Are you still feverish, lass? There's nothing there."

I sighed, frustrated with the poor eyesight I'd always recognized in adults. Now I realized my sharper eyes and ears were not due to youth but probably to Ilvani blood.

"Trust me … there's a patrol up ahead. Three or four helmets."

He squinted, shaking his head. "Going or coming?" He still looked doubtful.

"How can I tell?" I snapped. "*You* can barely see them." I paused, watching for a bit. "Going, I think." I let out the half breath I'd been holding.

I let Nag walk forward just to stop his restless shifting, and Rhoan's mare fell into step beside me.

"Should we leave the road?" I asked, looking around. The countryside was fairly flat — easy to cross — but lacking in cover.

He shook his head. "That would certainly call attention to us. We stick to the road, like all other innocent travellers."

"But …" I began to protest.

"And we sing. Do you think your voice is any less effective just because there are soldiers involved?"

I shook my head, swallowing umbrage and worry at the same time.

"And if we're going the same direction, we won't need to cross paths at all."

That was a good plan as far as it went. I kept my eyes on the road ahead, holding Nag to a pace that never gained on the sparkling glints of armour ahead of me.

The sun rose and crossed the sky's axis while we kept our uneasy distance behind the armoured riders. It was up to me, with my better vision, to maintain the space. Between the glare of the sun in my face, the heat of it on my head, and the strain of maintaining a constant melody just below full song, my head-ache was pounding.

"We should stop now. Let the horses graze," I said. "And we can rest in the shade of those oaks."

Rhoan shook his head. "Wait till they break."

"Why? If they get farther ahead, that's good—we'll catch up when they do stop."

"And if they break for longer than we do, do we stop again? I'd rather keep them in our—your—sight."

"What if they don't break at all?"

"Then we're sure to make Gleoran by nightfall."

That was little comfort to my aching head. I returned my eyes to the road ahead and breathed my relief.

"They've stopped."

He peered down the road. "Are you sure? There seems just as much dust in the air."

"Of course I'm sure," I snapped. "You can see the horses milling about. That's why there's more dust."

I kicked my feet from the stirrups, ready to dismount, but

something about the cloud of dust made me look again. Was it just that some of the horses were turned sideways or …

"There's more of them!"

Rhoan was already on the ground. "What do you mean, more?"

"I mean there's more horses, more riders … at least twice as many. And they've stopped up ahead.

"Brandishear Patrol." He frowned, thought a second, and swung back into the saddle. "I guess we find out now how good your disguise is, lass."

I opened my mouth, but my throat was dry. Sure enough, the Aerach patrolmen we'd been following turned their horses back, having exchanged reports with their Brandishear counterparts.

"I can't." The words came out a barely audible croak.

Rhoan was gallantly striking up the harmony, and he made encouraging gestures while I shook my head.

He broke off. "Well then, lass, the song's only sugar coating on the disguise," he said kindly. "You look little enough like the handbill these days."

His encouragement merely dribbled off the wall of fear I felt growing around me. Another thought had struck. There was a chance — quite a good chance — the Aerach patrol contained riders from Teillai, any one of whom might know me, with or without a handbill.

With my voice gone, I couldn't even tell him this, and the flashes of sunlight off armour were growing larger and brighter with each constricted breath I drew. Yet another of those sense-less, panic-driven decisions I made so often drove me to yank Nag's head around, jump the grassy roadside ditch from a stand-still, and canter towards the stand of oaks on the right hand side of the road.

I could hear Rhoan's curse above the pounding of blood in my ears and looked back, relieved to see him mounting up to follow.

The oak trees were not nearly as densely spaced as they had seemed from a distance, nor so far from the roadside. Without checking to see if Rhoan followed, I wheeled again and sent Nag at a gallop toward the ravine between two low foothills.

The footing at the bottom was both rocky and muddy from spring rain, forcing me to slow to trot, and then to a walk. When at last I pulled up, Nag was huffing and snorting at the impromptu workout, and Rhoan's mare was slowly picking her way up the gully. From here the tops of the oak trees were still visible, but the road was hidden until it meandered into view farther east.

"They shouldn't be able to see us here," I panted when Rhoan caught up.

He was scowling. "Not from the road, no. But what if they turn off to find out why two riders went haring off into the hills? Which I'd certainly do if I were on patrol."

"You think they saw us?" I interrupted.

"By the time you made your made your mad dash, *I* could see them with my dreadful eyes. So yes, I'd say so."

The walls of fear pressed tighter, squeezing the breath from me.

"What do we do?" I whispered, feeling tears start.

"Sensible option: we ride back down. If they ask when we meet them, which we will do, I tell them my *daughter's* horse spooked and bolted. And we carry on our way."

"But we can't ..." I shook my head, trying to shake away the tears that wouldn't stop. "I can't sing the glamour anymore. I just can't." Though in truth, my voice, hoarse though it was, could probably have carried the charm if my heart were bolder. "And there may be … probably will be soldiers from Teillai. They'll *know* me …"

"And then what, lass?" he asked and reached over to put a gentle hand on my knee.

Nag was taller than his mare and standing upslope from her, so Rhoan had to look up to see my water-filled eyes and crumpled chin. "They'll take you home, where your family loves and cares for you. Is that so bad that you'd risk fleeing through the Kelerin hills with me instead?"

I couldn't answer. I couldn't tell him that I no longer *could* go home, with Doniver's death on my hands, and face Mother and Angeley. That I was no longer sure they would still love and care for me.

I only nodded. He sighed, patted my knee, and pushed past Nag, leading the way up the gully.

Irdaign's Chorus

Coming home to Teillai *after being away for one of Chanist's visits always seems like visiting a new province altogether. Or another world, just like this one but altered in unidentifiable ways, as if turned a fraction of a degree on its axis. I have never been entirely sure how the gift of precognizance works. That I can see things before they happen does not mean that all our lives are preordained. For if they were, what use would be the Sight? Things would roll out on the carpet of history and future with never a snag or dropped thread. Some things I have seen have never come to pass, as if by seeing I have altered the weft of history. And yet others I see are terrible, and I am powerless to prevent them. All I can try to do is soften the blows they have on the lives around me.*

Did I save Chanist from death at Welbirk? I did not see his death as I did the other three of his family, only felt a presentiment of danger that made me call him home before his sister, brother and father died, all within a week of one another. And did I save him for the good of the Ilmar, or for my own selfish reasons? If I had not, what other world might I be coming home to? Not one shifted a fraction of a degree, but one turned ten, twenty, or fifty degrees on its side? How can I ever know?

I sometimes feel that time is merely a construct and all that ever will happen already has, in its infinite possibilities. So perhaps the Teillai I left is not the one to which I come back, for something small has changed. A tiny, unforeseen choice has moved me from one future to the next one over. Why does this make me so uneasy? Does the need to hold the shuttle that weaves my family's threads grip so tightly that any small loss of control causes me worry?

I take a long measured breath as my carthorse slows to a stop in front of Osthegn's great gates. The stakes are high, yes, but surely I am not so important in the grand tapestry that I cannot allow other hands to cast a pass or two. Not all the times life has surprised me have been bad. Surprises, on the balance, have been as many parts pleasurable as otherwise. I wonder what surprises await me this time.

Hardin and his son *are sitting on overturned buckets, cleaning harness by the sunny south wall of the stables. Hardin jumps to his feet with a jangle and clatter as the leather and brasses tumble to the ground.*

He hands me down from the cart with such alacrity and deference I wonder for a moment if he has guessed my true relationship to the lady of the castle. No, I decide, it is merely the respect so many stablemen have for Leisanmira.

He holds my hand for a tiny instant after my feet have touched ground.

"It is good to have you back, Mistress Angeley."

"It's good to be back, Master Hardin," I reply, smiling at his kind and honest face.

"Wulf," he calls over his shoulder. "Quit dallying and unhitch Pashu." He swings up onto the buckboard, reaching out the cases and bags I have brought back from Aleran.

"Are these all going to your workshop, mistress?"

"Yes, but don't trouble yourself with them. The porter can deal with that."

"No trouble at all, mistress." He grins, tossing a sack over his shoulder and grasping two bags apiece in his great hands. "I'll take them straight over."

"And how goes it in the stable yard, Master Hardin?" I ask, slowing my usual stride to match his easy gait. "How's the filly doing?"

"Growing hand over hand." His smile stretches to his ears, crinkling the sun-cured skin around his eyes. "Aster's a good mother in spite of her snarly nature. Her Grace has ta'en an interest in them both."

"She has?" There it is: a complete and unforeseen happening. It is nothing of import in the grand weaving, just a thread I hadn't expected or seen before.

"Aye, the Duchess has a canny way with the pair of them——she's the knack of horses, no doubt."

"She's of the royal line of Brandishear. Horses run in her blood."

"Well, I'd swear there was Leisanmira in that touch of hers as well …"

My heart does a trip and double beat.

"… not just from her golden hair and sea-blue eyes."

I breathe, my thoughts scrambling around in my brain for the correct response. What is he implying? The breath calms me, and I realize truth is my friend here.

"Did you not know, Master Hardin? Her Grace's mother was Leisanmira."

He frowns. "I thought she was some small royalty of Brandishear——not that I know the Noble families, 'specially not outside Aerach. But still——Leisanmira? Are ye sure?"

I can see he is both pleased and puzzled. Puzzled at the incongruity of gipsy blood running in the veins of nobles, and pleased that he'd spotted her bloodlines like any good purveyor of horseflesh would. I am amused more than insulted. Proud, in fact, of my daughter's ancestry shining through.

"Her mother," I say softly, "was the Princess High Irdaign, first wife of Chanist of Brandishear, and quite fully and firmly of the Leisanmira."

He whistles, impressed perhaps at the height of her royal lineage, not widely known in Teillai. Or perhaps it is the other half of her blood that has his attention.

"Well, if that doesn't beat a dead donkey to life. No wonder she's such a beauty. Why, you could even be related."

My heart does its stumble again. That is too close to truth for comfort. I'm so preoccupied I nearly miss the compliment he's handed me. He places the bags at the door of my workshop and turns, asking where I'd like them put.

I let the question drift by, gazing at his honest, sun-worn features, and he is forced to ask again. I am utterly unaware of my answer, for I am caught up in the look he gives me.

Verse 16

Into the Wasteland

The ravine between the two hills narrowed before long, becoming clogged with small trees and undergrowth that forced us onto the hillsides. No longer able to play the average and stay in the ravine, we were forced to choose the left- or right-hand path. Rhoan looked back at me, leaving the decision resting on my saddlebow. The right-hand foothill was slightly less steep, with easier footing. But if we took that, we'd be keeping the gully between us and the west.

"Left," I said, without a trace of the hesitation I felt. "The vantage is better," I added in attempt to hide my real motive, which was to increase the distance between me and Aerach.

Rhoan didn't argue, just nodded and kicked his mare across the rivulet of water that ran along the ravine floor, heading up the rocky bank to the tuft-covered slope on the left.

The horses were lathered and puffing from the climb when the hill finally levelled out to provide us a vantage. To the north loomed a larger hill, a mountain almost, though dry and brush-covered, not lush and forested with a snowy head like the mountains of home. To the east was the lower hill, the one we didn't climb, and to the west a ridge skirting the larger mountain like a curtain wall around a massive keep, leading off to the maze of the Kelerin range.

The horses couldn't puff for long.

"Look." I pointed down the hill behind us.

That now-familiar and awful glint of metal in sunlight winked out of the tree-lined gorge. A single rider, and thankfully on the eastern slope.

I heard Rhoan let out a whooshing breath. "Not so good a tracker, then," he breathed. "But let's move before he spots us."

I drummed my heels against Nag's reluctant sides. He snorted, almost, but not quite, masking the distant shout. I looked back again. A rider on the opposite hill was pointing and calling … and someone answered. I had to know. I dragged Nag's head about and forced him back at a trot in the direction we'd come, just until I could look over the hillside. Sure enough, a second rider was on the same hill as we were, and moving as fast as his burdened horse could lunge upward.

I spun Nag back and kicked him into a canter, surging past Rhoan on the narrow ridge. "There's two of them," I yelled.

Cursing, Rhoan spurred his mare to catch us.

I leaned low over my saddle, one hand holding the reins as far forward as I could, giving Nag his head over the uneven ground; the other twisted in his mane, expecting a stumble or jump at any time that could spill me from the saddle.

The ridge was long and twisting, rising and falling like the back of a dragon. At several points Nag had to slow to a trot to negotiate the wild game trails that wove their way along it, and at many of these I caught sight of our pursuer flashing over the horizon and disappearing again. However, each time he appeared he was farther away. He was lightly armoured, but it was enough to slow him.

"Hold!" Rhoan shouted at last, slowing to a walk. Nag was only too happy to comply, despite my desperate urge to push on.

"Their horses can't keep the pace of ours," he said, echoing the useless reassurances my logical self kept repeating. "We can slow, at least for a bit."

I nodded with reluctance, acknowledging the truth of the statement and the need to rest our blown horses.

After walking two full sets of switchbacks, Rhoan allowed us to move faster. "Trot only," he said. "It's fast enough for this terrain, and they'll last longer."

"Should we head down into the trees?" I asked, looking nervously at the ever steeper shoulder that led into the thin pine forest now between us and the road.

"Not a bad idea—next down-ridge we get. Better than heading into that." He motioned with his head toward the badlands of the Sandhorn, which stretched out below us to the north.

Soon enough a side slope did lead down into the forest. Rhoan led the way, his mare cautiously zigzagging down the scree-strewn slope. The shoulder levelled for a bit, and widened, taking a gentler, almost road-like track as it entered the sparse but welcome shade of the pines.

The bay mare had just slipped into that shade when Nag's head shot up. At the same time I heard the clink and jangle, saw the terrible telltale flash again.

"Rhoan!" I hauled back on Nag, causing him to scramble for footing and almost slide off the shoulder. The gelding didn't want to go back up the hill, never mind at speed, but I pounded with my heels till he did. I couldn't even spare a glance backward as he lurched in great rock-scattering leaps up the hillside, me clinging to his neck like a burr in his mane.

I heard a horse behind me as we crested the hilltop, prayed it was Rhoan, and started off along the western track, only to come to a skidding halt. Coming towards us, in Brandishear blue and silver, was another horseman. And our first pursuer, in Aerach colours, was clearly visible to the east. They must have sent riders back to the Brandishear patrol.

Without asking, without waiting, I took my last open direction, sending Nag skidding down the steeper northern slope, straight into the badlands.

The air felt different almost the instant our horses' hooves started down the northern shoulder. The wave of heat, like a smithy furnace, rolled over us as the horses slid and scrambled down the rocky decline. Even when we entered the shade of the ravine bottom, there was little relief.

Shouts were audible from the ridge top, and I could clearly see both Brandishear and Aerach colours on the patrolmen who gathered there. Rhoan pulled up behind me in the shadowed side of the ravine, and we peered at the soldiers. Their horse's ears made a row of points against the horizon, mirroring the feathered treetops. The patrolmen weren't following us, or stringing their bows. Nor were they leaving. It seemed they were content to leave us to the mercies of the desert and the bandits who lived there.

I wanted to apologize to the bleak look in Rhoan's eyes. Instead, I said, "We could wait till they leave?"

He shook his head. "They won't. Oh, for certain some will report back to their way stations. But at least four will camp on that ridge — and patrol the ones on either side for the next several days."

"So where do we go?"

He looked north into the rutted and wind-blasted desert ahead of us. "Into that."

The dry hot air wrapped itself around me, drinking the last traces of moisture from my skin, my nose, my eyes. The horses, once lathered and sweaty from our frantic chase over the hills, were dry now, their coats bristly and caked with hardened dust and foam. They walked slowly, their heads low, stumbling on the cracked and rocky desert floor. Rhoan's part-Sandbred bay suffered less than Nag, whose black coat soaked in all the shadowless heat.

By all rights the water-laden air from the sea should have made this peninsula greener and more temperate than the land south of the mountains. But the immense forest of the Valnirata creates its own climate, which gathers moist air and recycles it over the Greatwood and its environs. Prevailing winds from the Clearwater send the sea air scudding past the Sandhorn, slipping sideways past the Kelerin hills and into Aerach's south-western reaches, leaving the northern reaches of Kelerin and the Sandhorn a region of bare red and grey rocks with swirling sand dancing beneath clouds that withhold their rain. It is inhabited by strong desert plants, hardy beasts, and people who have no better place to live.

Nag stumbled yet again, throwing me against the saddlebow. I took this hint at last and slid to the ground, feeling the oven heat of the sand and rocks through my boots. The air was even hotter this close to the ground.

One step, two, three, four … I counted in time to my foot-falls. Any distraction to keep my feet moving. It was boring, but all I could think of.

Rhoan, riding ahead, noticed me falling back and dismounted as well.

He didn't speak—just raised a questioning eyebrow at me. I nodded assurance that we were fine, and he turned north again, leading Talwis. No need to waste breath on talk.

The dark shadow of a large rock we had chased all afternoon was growing larger at last, though perhaps that was just the lowering sun stretching it. I looked back at the Kelerin hills behind us, with their taunting fringe of trees. They seemed smaller, and were so far off I could no longer smell the pines or taste the cooler breezes that trickled off them.

By the time we stumbled into the lee of the great rock, its shadow stretched across the ragged desert floor to three times its height: a welcome black blanket on the red-gold glare of late afternoon. A family of stunted, scraggly trees—no more than bushes, really—huddled at its base. Grooves etched in the rock showed where rainwater had converged and collected year after year, the channels carving a hollow side to the otherwise loaf-shaped mound. It was in this protected hollow, where trees thrived, if barely, that we found water.

It was no more than a puddle, two large strides across, shallow but clear, with a muddy border indicating it had been larger than this at dawn. Beyond the mud was cracked, dry clay, and beyond that bunches of harder, deep-rooted grass.

The numerous small animal tracks indicated the water was sweet. Moreover, it was the sweetest thing I'd tasted in all my life. Rhoan held the eager horses well away from the water, letting them graze while I refilled our four water skins. When at last we let the horses drink, they widened the muddy verge by a good foot.

"It wasn't always like this, you know." Rhoan used his shirt to wipe his wet face.

I looked at the arid land around us, relieved only by the tall upshoot of rock and the straggly bushes that survived in its lee.

"How do you know?"

He stretched his long legs out in front of him and began unlacing his boots. "Ancient legends say people lived here once — that the land had trees, and crops. There are even traces of buildings out here somewhere."

I frowned. Willits had been excessively diligent in stuffing Ilmar history into my head, but this was not familiar.

"You mean Ilvani — before the arrival of Ilmari?"

"No. Before the Ilvani."

"But they were here for thousands of years before the Ilmar migration."

He had his boots off and was splashing water onto his feet. I looked askance at the waste.

"Don't you think we should conserve the water?"

He shook his head. "This is a rainwater puddle. It ran off this mountain during the rains we suffered from last week. From the size of it, it will be gone by tomorrow anyway. Our canteens are full—enjoy it while you can."

I lifted a disapproving eyebrow but decided I'd take my own boots off as soon as the horses were groomed.

"What happened then, to those people—did they move, was there a war?"

He shrugged. "We don't know. They might have warred with the Ilvani. They might have moved when the land became barren. Or maybe some other calamity struck."

It irritated me, this uncertainty over something so vast as the disappearance of a civilization.

"We may never know," he added, only making it worse.

I untacked Nag, brushing the dried sweat out of his coat as best I could, and began picking the stones out of his feet. I let out a wail as I held up the gelding's off fore. "Look," I said, my chin quivering embarrassingly as I tried not to cry.

The hoof I held was still shod, but barely. Of the three nails that held the left side of the shoe on, one was loose, another was missing entirely, and a third had worked itself halfway out and bent over, so its square head pushed into the sole of Nag's foot.

Rhoan whistled, shook his head. "Damn me, I should have had him re-shod when we were in Werrancross. I'm so sorry, lass."

I dropped the hoof, and my tears began in earnest. Part of me, the childish part, wanted to latch onto Rhoan's self-recrimination and blame him; but I knew I had no one to blame but myself. I counted the weeks since I'd left home—too many. Nag's feet were far longer than they ought to have been, the hoof wall growing out over the shoes, and it was a miracle he hadn't cast a shoe before this. No wonder he'd been stumbling all day.

I grabbed one of the plentiful rocks and lifted Nag's foot to bang the one straight nail flush with the shoe once more. The hoof around the clinches was dry and crumbly, and there was no way I could re-clinch the nail I'd just re-driven, but it might hold a day or so. I slipped my knife under the bent nail, noting how Nag flinched when I dug the head out of his sole. It had created a bruise for certain, but at least it hadn't punctured the sole.

There was no way to salvage the nail, so I wiggled it with the crossbar of my knife. It came out far too easily. That left one nail badly clinched, holding the left side of the shoe on.

"Do you have nails?" I asked Rhoan, knowing already what the answer would be. His mare went barefoot.

He shook his head. "No, but we'll make something."

"Make … out of what?" I could feel an edge of hysteria creeping into my voice.

Rhoan rested his hand on my back between the shoulder blades. It was hot and uncomfortable, pressing the sweaty clothes to my back, but it was also oddly comforting, an echo of Ange-ley's reassuring touch.

"Something. We'll work out something. But for now, we need to rest."

Verse 17
The Sandhorn

I woke up with the first change in light, my body cramped from shivering. I had argued with Rhoan about the need to set up the tent in this hot, parched desert, but he was right: the heat from the ground had long since vanished, and the dry air held no warmth. I stuck my nose back under the blanket, breathing back my warm breath, and shifted closer to Rhoan, ignoring the nagging from my bladder.

There was a small square of canvas missing from the corner of the tent flap, sacrificed, along with one of Rhoan's bootlaces, to improvise the slipper that held on Nag's shoe. Through the hole I watched the sandy ground turn from black to blue to grey.

Just when I thought I might fall asleep again, Rhoan stiffened and then stretched, shaking cold droplets of our condensed breath from the tent.

He peered out the flap at the grey pre-dawn and swore. "We should have been up an hour ago." Tossing off his blankets, he crawled out of the tent. I followed, shivering, a blanket still wrapped around me.

Rhoan was already pulling up tent pegs, and I scrambled to retrieve our packs from inside before the tent collapsed on them.

"Breakfast?" I yawned.

The water hole had diminished overnight to an arm-span across, our tracks from yesterday already hardening in the drying clay. New tracks of desert fox, mouse, small bird, snake, and toad adorned the fresh mud beside the larger hobbled prints of our horses. Birds I could hear, invisible and distant, but of the other small night creatures there was no sign. How could they disappear so thoroughly in this treeless desert?

There was no time for breakfast, Rhoan explained. We needed to ride while the morning chill was in the air. I splashed a handful of muddy water on my face, wincing as it stung my sun-scalded cheeks.

A flash of kingfisher blue caught my eye, glowing and out

of place in the dawn grey. It was a spot no larger than an eagle coin, but it promised something larger buried in the clay. I scraped back the mud, revealing a larger and larger smooth blue surface. At no other time would I have been able to reveal it: yesterday the water had covered it: by this afternoon the clay would harden over it.

The surface rounded and went deeper into the dirt. Rhoan was urging me to finish packing the tent, but I was compelled now to unearth my find. At last he came to help and, with both of us scraping away at the sticky mud, we exposed the object: a pitcher of opaque blue glass, etched round the rim with unfamiliar patterns of script, and miraculously unbroken.

Rhoan whistled, shaking his head in admiration as the first rays of sun creased the horizon and set the jug aglow. I took it from him, wiping bits of clay from the incised script. It was writing—of that I was sure.

"It's not Ilvani," I said. "Where do you think it's from?"

He shook his head. "I wish I knew." There was an odd, hushed quality to his voice. "It's not Kavatir either, or from any of the outland nations I know of. And it's old."

"How do you know?"

"Look inside."

The inner surface of the jar, once cleared of the thick darker mud inside, was marked by criss-crossed black patterns.

"That's from decaying plants," Rhoan pointed out. "Water weed."

"So?"

"This little puddle couldn't sustain water plants. I doubt it has for centuries. The Sandhorn has been a desert like this as far back as recorded history shows."

"So …" I added up the dates of the calendar: 1600 from Empirical dates, and nearly as many in the pre-Empire days beyond it.

"I could be wrong." There was that odd quality to his voice again. "But if I'm not …"

"This jug is worth a lot."

"Much more than a lot. Something like this … proof of people here that long ago … clever people, to make something this beautiful. No, that is priceless."

I quickly put it on the ground, terrified of dropping something that had survived at least three millennia buried in the ground.

We stuffed it with an empty grain sack, wrapped it in one of Rhoan's best shirts, then nestled it in the remaining grain sack, hoping the oats would cushion any shock. That sack went across Nag's pommel, and I rode with a nervous awareness of our treasure resting just in front of my hand, which stole down to check on it every few strides. Nag's trot was rough enough at the best of times, and with his unevenness from the improvised canvas shoe and the rocky, trackless desert footing, I was in a constant state of worry that the bundle would come untied, or that his jolting trot would smash the vessel to dust.

Our shadows, stretching long and blue in front of us when we had started, had shrunk to small puddles of black. I begged Rhoan for a halt. It was an even more barren stretch of land we were now in. The foothills to the south were hazy bumps on the horizon, separated from us by a long gorge that had started as a small rift between the rockier ground and the smooth desert. Now it was the width of a river and the depth of a lake, with none of the longed-for moisture of either.

Nag was limping badly, and when I slid off I saw that the canvas boot had worn straight through.

"We can't rest here," Rhoan insisted. "No water, no shade, no wind."

"But he can't go on," I protested, holding the unshod hoof, which now sported a large chip out of the left wall and two spreading cracks on the right.

"Then we'll head there." Rhoan pointed to the gorge. "There may be a way down. Or at least some shade." He looked down into my despairing face. "You lead him halfway there, then we'll switch."

That journey of maybe half a league in the midday sun seemed to take longer than the six or seven leagues we'd travelled since dawn. I felt nearly as lame as Nag by the time Rhoan took over leading, and I mounted his mare at what was probably far less than the halfway point. I ended by sliding off and leading the mare, walking in what little shadow she cast, long before we reached the lip of the gorge.

And there, any hope of shade was dashed—as it would have been before this if we'd paused to think. For the gorge ran east-west and the sun was still high overhead. Even when it descended it would continue to shine on the northern face: the small slivers of shade lingering in the rock outcroppings of the southern wall were separated from us by the precipitous ravine.

Rhoan's face was now as desolate as I felt. For the first time it occurred to me we could die out here in this desert, with little food and less water. Or the horses could. This latter thought was the one that brought guilty tears to my eyes, and I leaned my head against Nag's too-dry, salt-stiffened hide.

We poured some meagre water into our mazers for the horses to sip and allowed ourselves a precious mouthful each.

I couldn't even voice the question "Now what?" though my face must have said it for me.

Rhoan's skin was red and parched despite the white cambric shirt he'd used to cover his head. The creases around his eyes and mouth were darkened with the dried muck of sweat and dust. My guilt expanded to include him as well as the horses. All this was my fault. So immersed was I in my self-pity, I barely heard him.

"Allaigna?" he repeated, shaking my shoulder. "If you can't see anything, we'll put up the tent here and wait till the sun lowers."

And what about the horses? Or when the sun travelled west and to shine straight in our faces?

I shook my head and peered down the length of the canyon, scanning in both directions for a way down. There were trees at the bottom, and every once in a while the ghost scent of moisture drifted up, making me hope for a river or at least a spring. But the edge at our feet was unrelentingly steep for as far as I could see westward. To the east, though, the canyon rose and the cliff edge melted somewhat. And was there, perhaps, a ledge sloping crosswise down?

But even if it wasn't a trick of the light, could the horses manage it? It would mean another half league of travel, back in the direction we'd come. It was so much more tempting to simply sit here waiting for darkness to come and save us. But then tomorrow we would be faced with the same choices, and even less water.

Rhoan couldn't see the hope that shimmered on the eastern horizon. Which left the decision on my shoulders. I rolled them back, feeling sand and dry sweat creak and scratch against my neck. I'd put Rhoan in this situation, and I would get him out.

"East," I pointed. "Half a league." My heart fell even as the words escaped my lips. "Maybe a bit less," I added to encourage us both.

At least as we turned our faces east, the sun now had to settle for our backs, and our dwarfish shadows led the way.

The shadows lengthened as slowly as our progress, footfall by limping footfall, back in the wrong direction. With each painful step my heart lurched, pulled by the green shores of Aerach—which I could now see as a distant smudge on the northern horizon—and repelled still by the desperate sense of flight that pushed me toward Brandishear. The dual forces left a void between my ribs, an ache so empty I would have filled it with tears if only there were enough fluid left within me to cry.

At last we approached the breach in the canyon lip. It was no more than a crumbled edge where the steep walls gave way to one that was gentler, but treacherous with scree. There was no safety there, or shade.

My parched eyes discovered a few last drops of water that muddied my vision. I sat down, head in hands, too dry to cry outright, too despairing to do anything else.

I had led us all this way back for nothing. The relentless sun still beat on us, but now our shadows stretched long and we would spend another night in this desert, this time with no water and no shelter from the nighttime wind and frost.

I could feel Rhoan's hand on my shoulder. His tall form shaded mine, so I didn't shrug him off.

"The land is more broken farther on, Allaigna." His voice was cracked and caked with sand. "We may simply need to go farther."

Farther? I couldn't possibly go farther. But then … all this was my fault.

I grasped his elbow in an unusual acceptance of support and allowed myself to be pulled upward. I nodded and limped onward.

§

You can't escape magic when it's in your blood …

When Allaigna was seven she almost sang her baby brother to sleep — forever. She may not be heir to her mother's titles and secrets, but she has inherited her grandmother's dangerous talent for singing music into magic.

Allaigna's Song: Overture is a love story, a family saga, and a coming-of-age novel that braids together the stories of daughter, mother, and grandmother.

ISBN: 978-0-9949565-9-0 (print)
ISBN: 978-1-98886500-3 (eBook)

Epic fantasy bestseller on amazon.ca
Pulp Literature Press

Allaigna's Song
Overture
JM Landels

PULP
Literature
JJ Lee
'The Man In the
Long Black Coat'

PULP
Literature
Carol Berg
'Uncanonical Murder'

PULP
Literature
Matthew Hughes
'The Devil You Don't'
Allaigna's Song: Aria

PULP
Literature
George McWhirter
'Stalk'

PULP
Literature
FANTASTIC
FRESH
FICTION
www.pulpliterature.com

THE ARTISTS

Ben Baldwin
Cover artist, Jinn
Ben Baldwin is a self-taught freelance artist from the UK who
works with a combination of traditional media, photography,
and digital art programs. He has been shortlisted for the British
Fantasy Award for Best Artist for the last seven years and has
also been shortlisted for the British Science Fiction Association Award for Best Artist. In 2013, he won Best Artist of the
Year in the annual This Is Horror Awards. His short horror
comic 'Bone Dry' with writer Roy Gray appeared in *Pulp Literature* Issue 18, Spring 2018. You can find out more about Ben
and his work at benbaldwin.co.uk and facebook.com/pages/
Ben-Baldwin/343132594365.

John Henry Friesen
End illustration, 'Away Game'
John Henry Friesen began contributing cartoons to the Steinbach,
Manitoba paper at age 14. He took a correspondence cartooning
course from Ohio, and later one from Art Instruction with Charles
Schultz. "John Henry's" cartooning is affiliated with TV series
including Skiddle Bits, Third Story, and Sesame Street. He has
illustrated book covers, created magazine illustrations and has oper-
ated a thriving sign business since the 1960s. He continues today.

Mel Anastasiou

Illustrator, 'Meat', and in-house illustrator

Mel Anastasiou loves drawing for *Pulp Literature* because she loves the stories she illustrates. She draws in black and white, working from imagination and inspired by details from Renaissance compositions. You can find more illustrations, as well as writing tips and news about her books and novellas, at melanastasiou.wordpress.com.

HALL OF FAME

These are the heroes — the Patrons and Pulp Literati whose monthly support helped bring you this issue. Please lift your glasses and give them a rousing cheer!

The Inner Circle
Jenever J Utsey

The Landlords
Adam Fout

The Innkeepers
Ada Maria Soto
Dana Tye Rally
Ev Bishop
Roger & Anne Anastasiou
A Bursewicz
Kevin Harris

The Cicerones
Sandra Vander Schaaf

The Bartenders
Keith Rydstrom
Alana Krider
Richard Gropp
Margot Landels
Ron Graves
Susan Lefeaux

Kristen Mah
Corey Reid
Michelle Balfour
Robert Bose
Sharon McAuley
Victoria McAuley
Dave Wayne
Scott F Gray
Abigail Bruce
Patrick Bollivar
Dietra Malik
Elaine McDivitt
Angela Dorsey
Joshua Pantalleresco
Emily Lonie

The Regulars
CC Humphreys
Marta Salek
Rina Piccolo
Leigh Matthews
Kim Harbridge
KT Wagner
Harmony Neal

Jenny Blackford
Jain Cairns
Catherine McArdle
Adelene Ellenberg
Lisa Gordon
Clarisa Rivera Starr
Michael Barrie
Exprmntle
Tom Jolly
Dave Charpentier
Leo X Robertson
Kristene Perron
Akemi Art
Jennifer Timer
Bruce Cherry
Anna Belkine
Adam Lein

The Clientele
Kathy Denton
Ray Hsu
Melissa Hudson

If you would like to join the ranks of these worthies you can become a patron on Patreon at patreon.com/pulplit, or join the Pulp Literati through our website at pulpliterature.com/join-pulp-literati/.

MARKETPLACE

Books

Advent *by Michael Kamakana* We thought we knew what the aliens wanted. Think again. pulpliterature.com/advent

Allaigna's Song: Overture *by JM Landels.* Music, magic, and the shaping of a hero. pulpliterature.com/allaignas-song-overture

Paperboy: A Dysfunctional Novel *by Bob Thurber.* Photography by Vincent Louis Carrella. shantiarts.co/uploads/files/thurber_paperboy.html

Stella Ryman and the Fairmount Manor Mysteries *by Mel Anastasiou.* Trapped in a down-at-the-heels care home. You'd be cranky too. pulpliterature.com/stella-ryman-and-the-fairmount-manor-mysteries

Trolls *by Kris Sayer.* A comic guidebook narrated by a giant-spoon-wielding troll hunter. tatterhood.bigcartel.com

The Writer's Boon Companion *by Mel Anastasiou.* Thirty Days Towards an Extraordinary Volume. pulpliterature.com/subscribe/the-bookstore

Bookstores

Book Warehouse 632 Broadway W, Vancouver, BC V5Z IGI (604) 872-57II bookwarehouse.ca

The Comicshop 3518 W 4th Ave, Vancouver, BC V6R IN8 (604) 738-8I22 thecomicshop.ca

Myth Hawker Travelling Bookstore Canadian authors·Canadian content·small and independent press mythhawker.ca

Phoenix On Bowen 992 Dorman Rd, Bowen Island, BC V0N IG0 (604) 947-2793

Village Books & Coffeeshop 130-I203I First Ave, Richmond, BC V7E 3MI (604) 272-660I villagebooks@shaw.ca

White Dwarf/Dead Write Books 3715 West I0th Ave, Vancouver, BC V6R 2G5 (604) 228-8223 whitedwarf@deadwrite.com

"*Myth Hawker has a crush on the underdog: the small press, the overlooked author, the independent bookstore, and the vast, undiscovered treasures of small-scale publishing.*"

Myth Hawker travels the length & breadth of Canada, popping up at conventions & festivals in every province, showcasing the work of small press & independent Canadian authors. Follow them online to see where they're popping up next!

www.mythhawker.com   @Mythhawker

HELP WANTED?

If you are a new writer, or a writer with a
troublesome manuscript,
EVENT's **Reading Service for Writers**
may be just what you need.

Manuscripts will be edited by one of EVENT's editors and receive an
assessment of 700-1000 words, focusing on such aspects of craft as
voice, structure, rhythm and point of view.

Visit **eventmagazine.ca** today

NEO-OPSIS.CA

Explore neo-opsis.ca for submission guidelines, issue and subscription purchases, advertizing rates, news, information, desktop images, art, reviews, industry links and assorted neat stuff.

Dear Geist...

I have been writing and rewriting a creative non-fiction story for about a year. How do I know when the story is ready to send out?

—*Teetering, Gimli MB*

Which is correct, 4:00, four o'clock or 1600 h?
—Floria, Windsor ON

Dear Geist,
In my fiction writing workshop, one person said I should write a lot more about the dad character. Another person said that the dad character is superfluous and I should delete him. Both of these writers are very astute. Help!

—Dave, Red Deer AB

Advice for the Lit-Lorn

Are you a writer?
Do you have a writing question, conundrum, dispute, dilemma, quandary or pickle?

Geist offers free professional advice to writers of fiction, non-fiction and everything in between, straight from Mary Schendlinger (Senior Editor of *Geist* for 25 years) and *Geist* editorial staff.

Send your question to advice@geist.com.

We will reply to all answerable questions, whether or not we post them.

geist.com/lit-lorn

GEIST

FACT • FICTION • NORTH of AMERICA

More from Mel Anastasiou

CONTESTS

Pulp Literature runs four annual contests for poetry, flash fiction, and short stories. For contest guidelines, prizes and entry fees, see our website, pulpliterature.com/contests.

THE RAVEN SHORT STORY CONTEST
Contest opens: 1 September 2018
Deadline: 15 October 2018
Winner notified: 15 November 2018
Winner published in: Issue 22, Spring 2019
Prize: $300

THE BUMBLEBEE FLASH FICTION CONTEST
Contest opens: 1 January 2019
Deadline: 15 February 2019
Winner notified: 15 March 2019
Winner published in: Issue 23, Summer 2019
Prize: $300

THE MAGPIE AWARD FOR POETRY
Contest opens: 1 March 2019
Deadline: 15 April 2019
Winner notified: 15 May 2019
Winner published in: Issue 24, Autumn 2019
Prize: $500

$\mathcal{T}$HE HUMMINGBIRD FLASH FICTION PRIZE

Contest opens: 1 May 2019

Deadline: 15 June 2019

Winner notified: 15 July 2019

Winner published in: Issue 25, Winter 2020

Prize: $300

ℬECOME A PATRON OF PULP LITERATURE!

By supporting *Pulp Literature* on Patreon with $2 or more per month, you will be laying the foundation for a secure future for the magazine, as well as ensuring you will never miss an issue! Your subscription includes four big issues of short stories, novellas, poetry, comics and novel excerpts delivered to your door or electronic mailbox each year.

Find us at patreon.com/pulplit
If you prefer to subscribe through our website go to pulpliterature.com/subscribe.

Or you can send a cheque with the form below to:
Subscriptions, Pulp Literature Press, 21955 16 Ave, Langley BC, V2Z 1K5, Canada

---

Don't miss an issue!

❑   **Send me 2 years (8 issues) at the special rate of $90** (save $30)*
❑   **Send me 1 year (4 issues) for $50** (save $10)*
❑   **Send me 2 years of digital issues for $30** (save $9.92)
❑   **Send me 1 year of digital issues for $17.50** (save $2.47)

Name: ____
Address: ____
City: ____________________________________ Prov. / State: __________
Postal code: ______________ Country:_______________________
Email: ____

❑   Payment enclosed
❑   Bill me
❑   New
❑   Renewal

Make cheques payable in Canadian funds to S. Pieters. Include email address for digital editions and Paypal billing, or subscribe at www.pulpliterature.com.

*for postage outside Canada add $16 per year in North America or $32 per year overseas.